‘Wilding’s writing is rich in humour, fantasy and sharp social observation.’

Bruce Bennett, *Contemporary Novelists*

‘The best of the talent emerging from down under.’

San Francisco Review of Books

‘The literature of challenge rather than the literature of escape.’

Chris de Bono, Melbourne *Herald.*

‘He is so exhilaratingly adept with narrative you cannot put the book down . . . Wilding’s pen is sharp as a rapier.’

Jan Meek, *Vogue Australia*

‘If, like most of us, you’ve begun to sense that life is not quite so simple, then maybe Wilding is exactly who you should be reading.’

David English, *Weekend Australian*

‘Wilding has steadily produced, for over thirty years, work of high and lasting merit . . . To be a writer like Wilding is to be whole in a sense that should never be lost, not as long as the written word appears between the pages of a literary book.’

Don Graham, *Antipodes*

Also by Michael Wilding

Aspects of the Dying Process
Living Together
The Short Story Embassy
The West Midland Underground
Scenic Drive
Marcus Clarke
The Tabloid Story Pocket Book (ed)
The Phallic Forest
Political Fictions
Pacific Highway
Reading the Signs
The Paraguayan Experiment
The Man of Slow Feeling
Dragons Teeth: Literature in the English Revolution
Under Saturn
Great Climate
Her Most Bizarre Sexual Experience
Social Visions
The Radical Tradition
The Oxford Book of Australian Short Stories (ed)
This is for You
Book of the Reading
Somewhere New: New and Selected Stories
Studies in Classic Australian Fiction
Wildest Dreams
Raising Spirits, Making Gold and Swapping Wives: The True Adventures of Dr John Dee and Sir Edward Kelly

MICHAEL WILDING

ACADEMIA NUTS

WILD & WOOLLEY

Academia Nuts

ISBN 0 909331 94 4

Printed and published in Australia in 2002
Wild & Woolley Pty Ltd
P.O. Box 41, Glebe NSW 2037

FIRST EDITION

Acknowledgments
Some episodes originally appeared in
Antipodes, Critical Survey, DotLit, Imago,
Oasis, Overland, Social Alternatives and *Southerly*.

Layout and design by Vulgar Enterprises
Cover photographs and design by Pat Woolley

CONTENTS

To Christopher Bentley

1

Last Campus Novel

'People keep coming up to me and asking when am I going to write my academic novel,' said Henry.

'I'd have thought all your novels were pretty academic,' said Dr Bee.

'What do you mean?'

'In the nicest possible sense of the term, of course,' said Dr Bee. 'Not destined for the *salon des refusés*.'

'My university novel,' said Henry.

'That would be a good title,' said Pawley. 'A tentative post-modern evocation of Gorki. With a fictional qualification. *My University Novel*. Possibly realist, but not at all socialist. Right for the times.'

'You may mock,' said Henry, 'but they come up and ask me when I'm going to write it.'

'Informers,' said Pawley.

'They offer me information. Stories. Scandals.'

'Provocateurs,' said Pawley.

'They believe that literature could do something,' said Henry.

'Who at this university believes that literature could do something?' asked Dr Bee.

'The university police. They believe it does harm,' said Pawley. 'They're setting you up, Henry. They report it all back.'

'Back where?' asked Henry.

'Back to the Vice-Chancellor. The Pro-Vice-Chancellor. The Deputy Vice-Chancellor. The Chair of the Professorial Board. The Dean. The Sub-Dean. . . .'

'Senior management we call them now,' said Dr Bee.

'Haven't you notice how academic jobs are being abolished but the campus security service has expanded and expanded?' said Pawley.

'How do you know they're security?' asked Henry.

'Anyone who comes suggesting you write a novel has to be suspected, Henry,' said Dr Bee.

'You know them by their shoes,' said Pawley. 'They're always behind the times, in fashion, in culture, in literary taste.'

'Indistinguishable from our colleagues,' said Dr Bee.

'What do you mean behind the times?' said Henry.

'Asking you to write your campus novel. Don't you feel that by the time you come to publish it, the campus novel will be something from a vanished era?' said Pawley.

'No,' said Henry.

'With the universities degraded and destroyed, what sense will there be in a university novel?'

'What sense was there ever?' asked Dr Bee.

'A dead form,' Pawley went on.

'The great forms of the past didn't deal only with the present,' said Henry. 'Take the epic.'

'Surely modesty forbids,' said Dr Bee.'

'Homer wasn't writing about the contemporary.'

'So you see your work as a modern *Iliad,*' said Dr Bee.

'The fall of Troy. The end of a civilisation. Yes,' said Henry.

'Or *Paradise Lost*,' Dr Bee added. 'The loss of innocence.'

'Absolutely.'

'A small thing but your own.'

'It won't be that small,' said Henry.

'It will contain multitudes, no doubt,' said Dr Bee.

'Yes.'

'And what will you put in it?' asked Dr Bee.

'In it?'

'What inseparable content would you find for the classic form?'

'This,' said Henry. 'All this.'

There it was, their world lay all before them.

The deserted common room. The chipped cups. The worn, unfigured carpet.

'There's not an awful lot here,' said Pawley. 'I think you need more than the common room.'

'The university as such,' said Henry.

'You'd better hurry,' said Pawley. 'It's all being out-sourced. There's hardly anything left. The convenience store is the new model. A modem here, a terminal there. The virtual university. No tenured staff. No gross moral turpitude. No sad contagion of the gown.'

'I shall write about the university in decline,' said Henry.

'I think you might have left it too late,' said Dr Bee. 'Unless you offer it as an historical romance. Bodice rippers they used to call them in the trade, I think you'll find. Ah,' he sighed, 'those were the days.'

2

How To Get A Chair

'What you have to know,' said Dr Bee, 'is how professors get appointed.'

'How?' asked the new chum, the short-term, non-tenurable, fixed contract level A appointment, here today, gone tomorrow, ave atque vale, never seen again.

'How indeed?' said Dr Bee.

The afternoon sun filtered through the dust motes of the common room.

'Take our own illustrious examples.'

'Illustrious,' snorted Lancaster. 'I was lunching in Kings. "Who are your professors?" they asked. I told them. "Never heard of them," they said.'

'But they knew you,' said Dr Bee.

'Well, yes, I was having lunch with them, of course they did.'

'Henry Lancaster, our airport academic,' said Dr Bee, introducing Lancaster to the new chum. 'He luncheth here, he luncheth there, he luncheth damn nigh everywhere. But he is known. Internationally. Illustriously. Indubitably.'

'Well you can't say anyone's ever heard of the Dead Hand.'

'The Dead Hand?' said the new chum, nervously, as if he might be gripped at the throat by it, or clamped into his chair by those mechanical arms much loved of the Jacobean dramatists no one read much any more.

'Your boss,' said Dr Bee.

'Yours too,' said Lancaster.

'Just mine?' said Dr Bee.

'Ours, then.'

'The boss of all of us,' said Dr Bee, 'from who we radiate like the spokes of a wheel of fire.'

'Wheel of fire?' said the new chum.

'Wilson Knight,' said Lancaster.

'Shakespeare,' said Dr Bee.

'I'm not with you,' said the new chum.

'I hope you're not against us,' said Dr Bee. 'Just because the Dead Hand appointed you, you don't have to be one of his five daughters.'

A 747 roared above them, drowning out any chance of conversation, showering a poisonous gauze of unspent aviation fuel over the university grounds and the suburbs beneath its path.

'Thought you'd've been up there,' said Dr Bee when it had passed.

'Not till next week,' said Lancaster.

'And then?'

'Conference in Brunei. "Literature and Internal Security."'

Dr Bee let his eyelids close like a sated lizard. 'You were asking how the Dead Hand was appointed,' he said to the new chum. And before the new chum could confirm or deny, he was telling him.

'It was like this.'

It was late one summer afternoon in the professorial board room. The blow flies blew in from the corpses in the medical school across the Vice-Chancellor's garden. The Vice-Chancellor himself had switched off his hearing aid and was dreaming of a knighthood. It was his dream, his only dream, he had dreamed it for twenty-five years and it still held him entranced. The external assessors on the committee were doing sums on their note-pads for the expense claims they would submit for their attendance. The Dead Hand sat there in impassive boredom, the secret of his success, not only bored himself but sucking in the boredom from the room, the very lifeblood of his non-being, sustained by boredom and boredom alone, emanating boredom and nothing but boredom.

'Where else,' he reflected, 'could I be so myself, where else could I be so part of my environment?'

They called in the candidates one by one.

Lancaster had been first.

'I have a vision . . .' he began.

'Thank you,' they said, 'next.'

Next was Bannerjee. They got the first word in with him.

'Aren't you ashamed of being such a difficult character?'

He blenched. He almost turned into a white man. If he'd prostrated himself before the committee and said, 'Sahibs and memsahibs, I do heartily repent my difficult character and I promise to be a good black servant of my imperial masters and mistresses' he might have had a chance. But the shock turned him white and lost him any chance of being a token ethnic appointee.

Then there was the ambassador's daughter. She nearly got it.

'I don't really want this job,' she told them. 'I'm just between publishing positions.'

'What's a publishing position?' asked the man from the non-cognate discipline.

'Sounds like the missionary position, politically corrected to avoid offending post-colonial susceptibilities,' the external from Religious Studies suggested.

'And I'm expecting a better offer from New York any day.'

She probably would have got it but when the Americans heard she'd been interviewed they figured she had to be good and fixed her up with something in Virginia overnight.

'I was in the bar that evening,' said Dr Bee. 'The Professor of French Letters was complaining. "It's so hard," she said. "I've spent hours reading all these applicants' publication lists. How can I get my own work done?"

'"Never mind the lists," I said, "what about reading the actual books and articles they've written?"

'"Impossible. There just isn't time. Nobody can do that."

'I knew then she'd not even read the lists. Only Lancaster and Bannerjee had written any books. The rest had nothing but a rag-bag of unpublished conference papers, certificates of attendance at training courses of the Centre of Profitable Teaching, membership of appointment committees. The Americans hadn't even bothered to supply the ambassador's daughter with a manuscript to put her name to.

'"The obvious thing is to short-list only people with short CVs. People who haven't done too much or written anything," I suggested.

'"Oh, we do," she said.

'"You don't want to get yourself bogged down with people who've got half a dozen books behind them. Too set in their ways."

'"Absolutely."

'"You want to go for people with promise. People with everything in the future and nothing behind them. Something to look forward to that hasn't been written."

'"I couldn't agree more," she said.'

The committee was at an impasse. They didn't like anyone they'd interviewed. The VC didn't mind much since it was only a job in Literature and it had given him a chance to sleep through the whole proceedings. But no one else liked what they'd picked out of the applications. They'd gone for reflections of their own mediocrity and were appalled when it was manifested in front of them.

'Thank you,' said Lancaster.

'Nothing personal,' said Dr Bee.

What should they do? It was a question no one dared put for fear of looking ignorant.

The Dean seized the moment. He was never one for leaving a silence unfilled.

'There are three alternatives,' he said.

'You can only have two alternatives, actually,' said Lancaster.

'I am merely reporting what was reported to me,' said Dr Bee.

'First, we can do nothing,' the Dean said.

'I think we can all agree on that,' said the VC, beaming and switching off his hearing aid again.

'We could readvertise.'

'How widely did we advertise?' asked the man from the non-cognate discipline.

'In the usual way,' said the Dean. 'There are budgetary constraints. We put a notice in the weekend paper. And the *University Mirror*, of course.'

'Internationally?'

'There wasn't time,' said the Dean. 'We had to move quickly. And thirdly,' he went on, even more quickly, 'we could proceed by invitation.'

'Ah, invitation,' they murmured, like young girls in a vicarage at the rumour of a party.

'Splendid idea,' said the non-cognate man. 'Why didn't we think of that in the first place?'

'Well we did,' said the Dean. 'At least, I did. But there were due processes to be gone through.'

'Of course. Due processes.'

'But we've gone through them.'

'Indeed we have.'

'Absolutely.'

'So I suggest, if I may -'

'Indeed.'

'Absolutely.'

'We move to move by invitation.'

'Ra-ra,' they said.

'Splendid.'

'Excellent.'

There was the sound of chairs scraping on the floor as they prepared to leave.

'A moment,' said the Dean.

'Of course.'

'Whom should we invite?'

'Ah.'

The chairs were scraped forward. Elbows rested on the table.

'Well, speaking for myself, only personally mind,' said the Chairman of the Professorial Board, 'I would have thought we need look no further than this room.'

'But you've already got a chair,' said the VC.

The Chairman of the Professorial Board gave a hearty laugh. 'Very droll. No, not myself, not this time, thank you, no, I would have thought we had an excellent candidate sitting here amongst us.'

The committee's eyes flickered round the table furtively, checking out possibilities.

'Edward, of course,' said the chairman of the board, 'we need look no further than Edward.'

'Edward,' said the Dean, tentatively, 'Edward –,' trying to enunciate the absent –, there were two Edwards amongst them, Deadwood Edward, Ed Wood and the Dead Hand, D. E. D. Hand.

The chair of the board beamed but the rest were paralysed by the uncertainty of it.

'Which Edward did you have in mind?' the Dean finally asked.

The Chairman gestured, reached out his hand.

'Why, this one of course, who else?'

'Ah, Hand,' they said, relief hissing out of them like air from a punctured tire, anybody, anything, they would have appointed a race-horse from the Veterinary school to have ended this tortured embarrassment.

'Should he leave the room while we discuss this?' asked the Registrar.

'The toilet's on the floor below,' said the VC.

'If you wish,' said the Dead Hand.

'Only if you need,' said the VC.

'Well, I don't think we have to detain anyone any longer anyway,' said the Chair of the Board.

'And that's how it was done?' said the new chum.

'That's how it's generally done,' said Dr Bee.

'Of course there is another way,' said Dr Bee.

The new chum waited for him to add, there's always another way. But he didn't. It lay there, unsaid, the more threatening for being unsaid, suggesting the worse rather than the better. This was not a place for assertions of the spirit of hope.

'I even considered it myself,' said Dr Bee. 'Women used to be able to retire at 55 on a full pension. At the time it seemed worth considering a sex change to get out at 55. But Deadwood Edward beat me to it.'

'I don't think I know him,' said the new chum.

'That's because he's a she now. A few hormone shots, a quick slice of the knife, and Deadwood Edward became Deadwood Edwina. Less euphonious but no less sterile.'

'A masterly stroke,' said Lancaster.

'Mistressly,' said Dr Bee. 'Perfectly timed. Chimed in with equal opportunity. Career advancement for women. No matter that you'd never written anything or thought anything, discrimination has held you back, discrimination shall send you forward. No one keener that Edwina. Up the slippery slope she went. The gay lobby loved her. They established a centre for transsexual studies. Far more progressive than the gay and lesbian studies every other university had. Made Edwina the patron, or matron as she insisted. Lobbied for her advancement. The Dead Hand may have got his chair but Edwina effortlessly vaulted over him, riding on the backs of the women's movement and who knows what anatomical support of the gays. Aspro in a matter of days, then professor, then PVC.'

'PVC?' asked the new chum.

'The plastique of management. Pro-VC. Decorated for services beyond the call of duty. A Chancellor of vice all but in name. But soon to be, no doubt. A fully paid-up member of the kakistocracy.'

'And all your idea,' said Lancaster.

'All I conceived was a scheme for early retirement,' said Dr Bee. 'Promiscuously mentioned over morning tea. Deadwood Edward's ears pricked up. What a mass of undifferentiated quasi-erectile tissue that creature was. I'd learned never to mention a literary idea in his presence since he'd plagiarise it in an instant, ears like Venus fly traps, and then pour it out as a shapeless excretion of fly-blown fly juice onto some unsuspecting journal. Generally everything was rejected but once a decade he'd score a hit. So usually I was careful. But this. I could see no publishing potential in it. Little did I dream . . . .'

'You could still do it,' said Lancaster. 'It doesn't stop you going ahead with it.'

'They've changed the retirement rules,' said Dr Bee. 'First thing Edwina did on her equalisation committee. Progress and equality. Now women have to go on as long as men.'

'How long is that?' asked the new chum.

'No one knows. Compulsory retirement has been abolished.'

'I think you should still do it,' said Lancaster. 'Nothing to lose.'

'Speak for yourself,' said Dr Bee.

3

Harassment Tribunal

Dr Bee was visibly palpitating. From behind it wasn't possible to tell whether he was chuckling with delight or seething with rage. It was no more possible to tell from in front. The red glow suffusing his cheeks could have indicated either. Even if you asked him it wasn't certain there would be any reliable explanation.

'Are those tears of joy or an asthma attack?' Lancaster asked him, taking out his notebook, ever the campus novelist. 'I've never observed a fit before. Not at close quarters. Let me write the details down. Might come in useful. A bit of the old verité.'

Dr Bee beamed at him with bilious rage.

'I am reading the sexual harassment guidelines,' he said.

'To see if there's anything you haven't tried?' suggested Lancaster.

Dr Bee fixed him with a basilisk stare.

'Offensive looking,' he said. 'I experience offensive looking every time I make inadvertent eye contact with one of my colleagues. Let alone when I stand in a lecture theatre and am gazed on by the horrible hordes.'

'How about shaving?' asked Pawley, who was bearded and didn't.

'As for unwelcome body contact,' said Dr Bee, 'I suffer that from my fat female colleagues whenever I try to collect my mail from the office.'

'Fat-ism,' said Pawley. 'Now you're adding that to your unreconstructed sexism.'

'Contact with the anorexic ones is equally distasteful,' said Dr Bee.

'You've been making a comparative study?' asked Lancaster.

'Generally I can prod the ones with wasting diseases out of the way.'

'Jab them with your umbrella and deposit a pellet of castor oil poison in their calves.'

'No need,' said Dr Bee. 'Our colleagues are already at the limit of toxicity from their own substance.'

Happy days at morning tea. The door opening slightly, an eye peering through the crack, checking who was in, whether it was company to be avoided, indeed company at all, quick retreat, off to the take-away coffee stall. The sun streaming through the windows. Dr Bee basking like a lizard warming up to his operational body temperature.

The Head of Department swirled in, all business suit and blood red finger nails. She pulled down the blinds to eclipse the light and brought her tea and biscuits to the table.

Dr Bee glowered.

'What's that you've got there?' he asked.

'What's that?'

'That's what I'm asking you.'

'I'm not sure what you mean.'

'What are you eat-ing?' said Dr Bee, articulating each syllable like an artificial intelligence escaped from the language laboratory.

'What am I eating? A biscuit.'

'A choc-o-late bis-cuit,' he enunciated in the manner of a primary school reader.

'All right then, a chocolate biscuit.'

'But it is-n't all right,' said Dr Bee. 'Where did you get it?'

'From the biscuit tin, where do you think I got it?'

'I have nev-er seen a choc-o-late bis-cuit in the bis-cuit tin,' said Dr Bee.

'You must have missed out.'

'I must in-deed,' said Dr Bee. 'Have you ev-er seen a choc-o-late bis-cuit in the bis-cuit tin?' he asked Lancaster.

'Can't say I have.'

'Do you want some?' the Head of Department asked, offering him the chewed remnant.

He shuddered.

'Is that why you al-ways pull the blinds down?' he asked.

'I pulled the blinds down to keep out the sun.'

'So we would not be a-ble to see your choc-o-late bis-cuits?'

'You did see them.'

'I did in-deed,' said Dr Bee.

He brandished the sexual harassment guidelines.

'E-ven this doc-u-ment does not ass-ert a gen-der based al-lo-ca-ti-on of choc-o-late bis-cuits.'

'An oversight,' said Lancaster.

'Oh really,' said the Head of Department.

'Or is it one of the priv-il-eg-es of off-ice? Part of the Head of De-part-ment all-ow-ance?'

'It's just a chocolate biscuit,' said the Head of Department.

'But is it?' persisted Dr Bee. 'Or is it the man-i-fest-a-ti-on of priv-i-lege and dis-crim-in-a-ti-on? Is it the em-blem of the New Un-i-ver-sit-y, part of a wo-man-a-ger-i-al pack-age, part of a secret pos-it-ive dis-crim-in-a-ti-on pro-gram for the Spec-i-al Ad-min-is-tra-tive Ser-vice?'

He rolled up his sexual harassment guidelines, slapped them into his other palm, and rose decisively. At the biscuit tin he stopped, raised the lid, peered in, took a last meaningful survey of the room, and left.

'What is this,' said the Head of Department, 'about you holding classes in the dark?'

'I thought you would like it,' said Dr Bee.

'Why should I like it?'

'Do you not always close the common-room blinds when you come in?'

'To keep out the glare of the sun.'

'Absolutely,' said Dr Bee. 'I was simply in accord with department convention.'

'That can't be why you're doing it.'

'Absolutely,' said Dr Bee, 'not at all.'

'Then why are you doing it?'

'Harassment guidelines,' said Dr Bee.

'In what possible way can that be following the harassment guidelines?'

'Unseemly looking. Offensive gazing. Lascivious leering,' said Dr Bee. 'Only one way to stop all that. Put out the lights and then put out the lights. Then nobody will be able to see any other body. No more offence will be given.'

'Well put the lights back on.'

'As you wish,' said Dr Bee. 'I was but a guide dog trying to follow the guidelines. Dig out the subtext.'

'What subtext?'

'The subtext of the covering note. "These are to be implemented. H. O. D."'

'I sent that. There was no subtext.'

'I assumed you sent it,' said Dr Bee. 'Who else? I just followed the H. O. D.'

'Head of Department,' said the Head of Department.

'Oh,' said Dr Bee.

'What else could it mean?'

'Well,' he said, 'obviously nothing. Nothing will come of nothing. It's just that in my shorthand H. O. D. has always stood for *Heart of Darkness*. Being in a Department of Literature, as it were.' He beamed like an emissary of light. 'I thought it was one of those coded instructions to save electricity and close your eyes. You know, Switch off, sleep tight. Save power and stop looking. Kill two birds with one stone, as it were. Using birds in the nicest non-gender-specific way, of course.'

'How can you outlaw sex with students?' said Pawley. 'I always thought it was one of the perks of the job. Like free stationery.'

The Head of Department puffed up.

'Stationery is issued only for administrative and teaching-related work.'

'Well it's all teaching-related work,' said Pawley. 'Keeping in touch with the student body. Contact hours as we call them now.'

'People are becoming far too casual about these matters,' the Head of Department went on.

Pawley nodded sagely.

'In fact I'm thinking of instituting a charge for it,' the Head of Department went on.

'For sex with students?' choked Dr Bee. 'What, an across the board fixed fee? Or an hourly rate?'

'For photocopying and stationery.'

'Voyeurism and passive massage,' said Dr Bee. 'Surely we can do better than that.'

'One of the reasons for convening the sexual harassment board,' said the Head of Department, 'was to deal with complaints about offensive language and sexual innuendo. You may find yourselves brought before it.'

'Really,' said Dr Bee. 'I should be so lucky. Strict correction administered. Experienced governess offers discipline. When can I come? As it were. No subtext intended.'

The Head of Department sucked at her morning tea in scalding haste.

'I can see it,' he said, his eyes rolled inward like a cane toad over-full of Spanish flies. 'It will be like the old church courts. A scale of charges. Two pounds thirteen shillings and fourpence for fornication, three pounds six shillings and eightpence for adultery, rather more for incest. They called them fines but all the courts had their string of willing workers who would entice you. It was really a sort of deferred payment. Hire purchase. You paid them cash down for sex, and then you made a second payment to the courts for conviction. It financed the church, why not us? Solve the funding crisis. A perfect convergence of the authoritarianism of the medieval church with the monetarist free market model. I say -'

He refocussed his eyes from their avoidance-of-unseemly-looking mode and turned to the Head of Department. But she had left. Everyone had left.

'Why are we waiting?' asked Dr Bee. 'We have the sexual guidelines in place, why haven't we caught anyone? We have a harassment tribunal appointed, why are we so lax? When are we having our public hangings?'

'Public hangings, pubic hangings,' muttered Lancaster, surreptitiously giving issue to the now outlawed traditional campus novelists' foreplay. 'Don't we need a trial first?'

'Oh, I don't know,' said Dr Bee. 'This is the modern world. As long as we have a victim we can surely just get along with things. Trials are so unreliable. He might get off.'

'"He"?' said Lancaster. 'I thought the guidelines required non-gender-specific pronouns.'

'Not in cases of sexual harassment,' said Dr Bee. 'It's always a he in cases like this. That's the whole point of it.'

And then the word went round. We have a charge. Someone had made a complaint. There was tight-lipped joy in the women's gym.

'We rate at last,' said Dr Bee. 'How can you be a serious university in the modern age without a sexual harassment case? No one would believe in us. They'd say the Heart of Darkness wasn't doing her job. We'd all be blamed for failing to flush out the offenders. They'd say we were covering up. Now we can hold up our heads, stand up tall, though not erect. Don't want to be thought to be going too far. That's what bad girls used to do in my schooldays, go too far.'

'And your allegation,' said the Head of Department, 'is that Professor Rowley made advances to you.'

'Oh yes. Not just advances,' said Ms Chung. 'He advanced well beyond advances. But then he withdrew.'

'He withdrew. Are you saying this was his, ah, are you saying he was not, ah . . .?'

'Oh yes, he was using a condom. He didn't want to catch anything and give it his wife. All the time I said there is no need, I take the pill, I am healthy, in my country we have no diseases, I can show you my certificate of health. But he would never listen. He always wore a condom. Even when we didn't make love he wore a condom. I said, why do you carry a box of condoms around everywhere? He said he was a boy scout. Be prepared, he said, he was very proud of being a boy scout. Scouts' honour, he would say when I asked him if he had been sleeping with his wife. No, scouts' honour.'

'Let us get back to the charges. You allege he made advances, more than advances, and had a sexual liaison with you. Did he use his office to gain these favours?'

'Oh sometimes. Sometimes his office, sometimes his car, sometimes a motel, but he was afraid he might be seen in a motel, he was always afraid of being seen by colleagues. He said they all used the Campus Motel. I think there was maybe a special academic union afternoon rate.'

'What the Head of Department means is did he use his academic position to demand sexual favours?'

'Oh he used many positions. I don't know which was the academic position. He told me about the missionary position. He said in my country I wouldn't know about that. And the post-colonial position. That was very interesting. That was a first for me.'

'Please, what we mean, I think, was, did his being your tutor have an influence on you?'

'Oh yes. He would read me poems. John Donne. Elegy nineteen. "On going to bed." You know. And "The Rape of Lucrece." Oh very much so. And *Moll Flanders.* And *Emma.* Oh yes, I think all this was very influential. "Truth lies between her legs and so do I." That was a modern poem I think. And e. e. cummings. "She being brand new," you know. And "Naming of Parts."'

'And you feel this swayed your judgement?'

'Oh well, I think if one has a sound ideological analysis one's judgement will not be swayed by simple rhetoric. I think they were good works of literature, yes. But just because he wanted to make love after them I do not think means they are necessarily better works than many others. We often disagreed on this.'

'And this went on long?'

'Well sometimes he came quickly but often.'

'How long a period did this relationship continue?'

'Not very long,' she said, 'not long at all. Almost no time.'

'Well how long would you estimate. Days? Weeks?'

'Oh yes, last year, yes, but then this year suddenly nothing.'

'He abandoned you?'

'Shamefully.'

'And he made no further advances?'

'Never. He would not agree to anything. I would see him in his room and he would claim he had to leave. I would phone him up and he had his number changed. He refused to make any more advances. Like I said, he withdrew.'

'I'm not sure that . . . .'

'He behaved most shabbily. He went back to his wife and refused to see me. Not even twice a week. I said, I am willing to share you with that dreadful woman, why can't she? How can you do this? I told him, you behave like this, I must make a case. I shall go to arbitration. You say this is a fair country, then we will get a fair judgement. He withdrew and abandoned me. He ran away overseas.'

'These are very serious allegations, Ms Chung, that a member of staff was regularly having sex with you a student.'

'I was not a student, no. He was the student. I taught him everything. Now he goes back and teaches his wife. I give him all the secret techniques and what does he do, he betrays me with his wife. I told him, you are a typical imperialist, you call yourself post-colonial but it is no different, you come in like a spy in the night and steal our secrets and take them back to your white women, so has it ever been. You are like the opium traders, but do you bring any opium, no, you expect me to bring the opium, I bring you everything.'

The Head of Department made a last attempt to get the tribunal back on track.

'Now let us get this clear,' she said, 'you are alleging that Professor Rowley abused his position and had sexual relations with you, is that right?'

'No, that is not right, what I am complaining is that he refuses to have sex with me any more. I demand equal opportunity. I insist on my equal rights. I demand that he returns from overseas.'

Dr Bee staked out the tea line. The biscuit line. He hovered beside the notice board studying forthcoming conferences with one eye and watching the queue with the other. 'Literature, Law and the Body.' 'Cross-Dressing in Renaissance Drama.' 'Beyond Politics.' Each observation was punctuated with an involuntary grunt. He absorbed it all like a frog in mud, a crocodile on Nilus' slime. It appalled him. Everything appalled him.

When the harassment committee emerged for tea, shaken, he sidled up. The tea-person slipped a couple of chocolate biscuits into the tin and held it out to the Head of Department.

'Thank you,' said the Head of Department, taking them. They were on top after all.

'See,' said Dr Bee, 'there you are, chocolate biscuits.'

'That's what they look like,' said the Head of Department.

The harassment committee craned their necks round.

'Why?'

'What do you mean, why?'

'Why do you get the chocolate biscuits? What discrimination is this?'

'Anyone can have chocolate biscuits,' said the Head of Department.

'No they can't. There aren't any. Look.'

He seized the tin, brandished it at the queue.

'No chocolate biscuits before you came, no chocolate biscuits after you've been.'

The Head of Department looked baffled.

'So much for equal opportunity.'

The queue blenched at the phrase.

'This is what you should be looking at,' said Dr Bee. 'What

does your harassment tribunal have to say about this?'

'I really don't know what you're talking about,' the Head of Department said.

The tea-person brought out a packet from beneath the counter.

'Did you want one dearie? I know how much the Head loves them so I always keep a few back for her. But if you've got a sweet tooth too . . . .'

Dr Bee's teeth looked anything but sweet. They visibly sharpened.

'Go on, dearie,' said the tea-person.

'He only wants equal opportunities,' said Lancaster. 'It's just like our student complainant. Share and share alike.'

The student complainant stuck her head round the common room door.

'Oh Dr Bee,' she called out, 'could you spare me some of your valuable time?'

'All this and chocolate biscuits too,' said Lancaster.

4

Think of a Book

Some things were too painful to write about. It was true, to a degree, that writing about them gave a release, some how neutralised the pain, buried it, and then it was forgotten. Indeed, Lancaster found, once he had written about anything it tended to be forgotten. It was a way of elimination. Directed amnesia. But the university: it was too painful to begin on. A grief too deep for words. He sat there, looking at his novelist's water view. The leaden sky was reflected in the leaden sea. Surely it was the mood in which to write about the university. But he couldn't do it. The body resisted. The mind resisted. The hand would not hold the pen, the computer froze. Some characters should no more be written about than the art of murdering without pain. Why without pain? Why not without detection?

He stopped himself. This was what happened every time. His mind wandered off. Now he was about to get up and find what Dr Johnson actually wrote about characters who should not be written about, and then he'd think about writing a learned note or a keynote address or something and another day's fiction writing would have gone.

He tried everything. He tried the post-modern and wrote about being unable to write about it. The university. He had pages of writing about being unable to write about it. The university. He could put them all together and call them a novel. There were enough pages. For a post-modern novel. But the body refused. The mind went numb. A grey drizzle curtained the view.

Where did it go wrong? He was asking himself novelists' questions even when he couldn't write novelists' answers. Sexual harassment legislation. As soon as that came in a cloud of fear spread across the campus, like nerve gas from a U. S. Army funded research project. No one wanted to be seen within a hundred yards of a student. No more 'come into my office and we'll talk about it.' No more 'why don't we walk across to the union and have a coffee?' No more 'what about following this up in the pub?' No more, no more. Now it was the company of colleagues and everyone found it insupportable.

And cut off from the young, the supply of fresh blood terminated, they became like dusty old Draculas, not even getting out of the coffin at night, just lying there inert amidst the post-Gothic of it all.

For a while they had sat together in the faculty club at lunch time. The Dead Hand clamped onto a plate of club sandwiches which he munched through, silencing all conversation. Basilisk days. All of them sat there in mutual antipathy, caught in some sudden ice age chill and now bonded together in an iceberg locked into the polar wastes.

In the end Dr Bee came up with a trick. He had been closely observing the dynamics, what it was that impelled people suddenly to leave, a rending clash of tearing ice as they broke free and rushed out of the door.

'I think it's books,' he said to Lancaster on the way over. 'I'll try it with one of yours.'

The Dead Hand fanged through his cheese and gherkin and spam. Dr Bee sat with his coffee. He never ate with them. The Count of Monte Cristo principle. Lancaster poured down the red wine. The Head of Department and her latest protegé Philippa munched through their croissants and foccaccia and cottage cheese and rocket.

'I was reading one of Henry's novels last night,' said Dr Bee. 'Absolute insomnia. Three a.m. and not a wink. So I picked up a signed copy of *The Last Degree.*'

'Meeting,' said the Head of Department, wiping her face with a tissue and leaving a half-eaten croissant dead on the plate, the cream-cheese coagulating round its edges.

'I'll come with you,' said Philippa.

Before they were at the door the Dead Hand had cranked into motion.

'Bank,' he said.

'Organ bank? Blood bank?' asked Dr Bee.

Lancaster sat there somewhat ashen. A frequent shade.

'Am I so hated?' he asked. 'Despised and rejected of men?'

'Yes,' said Dr Bee.

'Do they loathe me so much?'

'Not you,' said Dr Bee. 'Books.'

'My novels?'

'Just books. Books in general. Books in particular. Your novels or anybody else's novels. All books are the same to them.'

'Books?' said Lancaster.

'Books,' said Dr Bee.

They tried it the next day. The scenario pretty well unchanged. Deadwood and the Dead Hand chewing across at each other. A couple of other sycophants. The icy silence.

'Read any good books lately?' Dr Bee asked.

There was a stir, the soft susurrus of shattering bonds, distant ice cracking, the pent up ocean ready to surge.

'I read that Chekhov you recommended,' said Henry. '"A Boring Story."'

'Duty calls,' said Deadwood Edwina, rising up.

'Bank,' said the Dead Hand.

'Bank again?' said Dr Bee. 'Being blackmailed or something?'

'Got to see a student,' said first sycophant, exiting right.

'Me too,' said the second, following.

Within seconds the table was empty except for Henry and Dr Bee.

Lancaster still could not quite believe it. He thought it might have been to do with the content of "A Boring Story." Not just books generically.

'No,' said Dr Bee. 'They never read. They wouldn't know what it was about.'

They tried it again later in the week. They tried it out for the next fortnight. It always worked. Mention a book. And off they all went.

Dr Bee sat behind piles of stacked books, ranked like scud missiles in the desert.

'Henry,' he called out as Lancaster came in, 'could I get you to sign some of your works?'

A smile of authorial satisfaction glimmered before it was swept away by authorial doubt and suspicion.

'Sign what?'

'Your books,' said Dr Bee. 'I bought them at the library. They were selling them off.'

'My books? Selling them off?'

'They must have been the multiple copies you ordered for non-existent courses to try and boost sales.'

Authorial fear and shiftiness competed with authorial rage.

'Why are they selling them off?'

'They're clearing the shelves,' said Dr Bee. 'Short of space.'

'It's like the purges of monastic libraries under Edward Tudor,' said Pawley. 'No one ever calls them purges. It's always shortage of space.'

'Why me?' said Lancaster.

'It's not only you,' said Dr Bee, somewhat impatiently. 'There are trestle tables full of books outside the library entrance. You're just one of the many. But I bought a copy of each of yours on the principle that the definition of a friend is someone who buys your books when the library throws them out so no-one sees your humiliation.'

'Then you bring them in the common-room and put them on display,' said Pawley.

'Nobody will come in,' said Dr Bee. 'They'll see a pile of books and back out immediately.'

Lancaster turned anxiously to the door. It seemed to move slightly, as if someone had peered in cautiously and then retreated.

'I brought them in here because I wanted Henry to sign them. I'd have brought more but I couldn't carry them.'

'More?' said Lancaster.

'I told you, they were multiples. They're throwing out anything that hasn't been borrowed on the grounds that no one uses them.'

'But what if someone puts them on a course next year?' said Lancaster.

'Then they're unavailable,' said Dr Bee.

'That's insane,' said Lancaster. 'Just because books aren't borrowed doesn't mean they shouldn't have been borrowed. Maybe courses are taught badly and the students aren't told to read anything. What happens another year when they are told to read something?'

'Maybe you order them again,' said Dr Bee.

'They'll be out of print by then so they can't be ordered again,' said Pawley. 'That's the beauty of the purge. They clear out books they know can't be replaced. It's practical mind-control. The new dark ages.'

'That's insane,' said Lancaster again.

'Not really,' said Pawley. 'They probably know about all your Serbian and Bulgarian and Cuban translations. Probably came up on a computer search somewhere. Red alert. Decided you were unsound. Purge. Eliminate. I agree it's disgraceful but it's not insane. It's all too sane.'

'You should go along in that case,' Dr Bee suggested to Pawley. 'If your theory is correct it will be a radical feast. A ready selected library of subversion.'

Pawley shuddered. 'Ugh, no,' he said. 'I can't bear all those dirty books.'

'I thought you had a soft spot for pornography,' said Dr Bee. 'Or a hard one, maybe. A child of the liberated sixties.'

'I mean dirty used books. Smears and stains. Ugh.'

'Semen? Blood?'

'Just coffee. Underlining. Highlighting. I don't know how you can bear them.'

'Oh, no problem with these,' said Dr Bee. 'These are Henry's books. Nothing like that. Virgin clean. No one's ever taken them off the shelves.'

Lancaster stormed out.

'You've upset him,' said Pawley.

'I don't think so,' said Dr Bee. 'He's just rushing across to buy up the other copies so he can present them to his foreign visitors. I should've bought up all the copies myself and then sold them back to him at a mark-up when he gets the library to re-order them.'

'Wouldn't have worked,' said Pawley. 'The new rules for ordering multiples are much tighter. He'd never get away with it again.'

It was true. All of it was true. It surpassed anything Henry could have fabricated in his fiction. The new rules. Henry striding across to the library. And outside it row upon row of trestle tables with row upon row of books culled from the shelves, a light drizzle falling on them, dampening their bindings, staining their pages. This was not a land of book burning, this was the free world, here books were just thrown out and damped down and sold for a dollar apiece.

The books remained on sale for a week and then they disappeared.

'Where have they gone?' asked Lancaster. 'What have they done with them? They haven't sold them.'

'You checked every day?' said Dr Bee.

'As I passed.'

'On your regular daily visit to the library?'

'Some of us read,' said Lancaster. 'Some of us research.'

'I thought your books were the product of felt experience.'

'Well they are.'

'Life lived to the hilt. Every moment a gift to the printed page.'

'Not every moment,' said Lancaster. 'There are times like these.'

'We don't merit even a reflective afterthought?'

'No,' said Lancaster.

He was determinedly ungenerous. The purging of the books had cut into the core of his being. For years he had felt that, awful as it was, the university was a base for literature. Continuities were transmitted. History preserved. Even when the teaching faltered the library was there. The books provided their own record. And now they were being thrown out.

'Why didn't they donate them to other libraries? Send them to universities in Asia.'

'Probably the Asian universities said, "No More" after the flood of gifts you've been sending them?'

'How did you know I'd been sending them gifts?'

'I check the mail,' said Dr Bee.

'My mail?'

'The outgoing mail,' said Dr Bee. 'Unavoidably. Every time I try to put a letter in the out box it's overflowing with jiffy bags consigned to remote outposts of empire. Books only. No commercial value. Gift of Henry Lancaster.'

'Better than having them pulped,' said Henry. 'They turn them into egg cartons if you don't buy them back. Can you believe it?'

'No wonder so many eggs are bad,' said Dr Bee. 'It's a wonder the eggs don't mutate and hatch out as aliens.'

'A lot of these libraries are very short of English language books.'

'But now they all have a complete set of the remaindered works of Henry Lancaster.'

'The Pacific rim is the fastest developing region in the world,' said Henry. 'It's only sensible to have one's books in the libraries of the region.'

'The future is theirs, comrade,' said Dr Bee.

'Absolutely,' said Lancaster. 'And if we don't get a foothold now we probably never will. We need to establish the English language holdings.'

'Salt the mine,' said Dr Bee.

'Absolutely,' said Lancaster.

The mystery of the missing books was soon answered. Land-fill. They were taken out in skips and dumped as land-fill on a reclamation site. Foraging students discovered them and brought them in to their tutors. 'Look at these library books we found. Are they first editions? Are they rare? Are they valuable?'

'I'm surprised they didn't burn them,' said Dr Bee.

'They're afraid of being accused of adding to global warming,' said Pawley. 'Pure cowardice. They should have stacked them in the quadrangle and had a public bonfire.'

'With martyrs on top?' asked Dr Bee.

It seemed appealing. Though they had some doubt as to who would be the martyrs.

'Henry?' said Dr Bee. 'Anyone who's written as many books as you ought to be burned on top of them. A sort of widow's suttee don't you think? Only proper in this post-book world.'

Henry had lapsed into a traumatised silence. The thought of his virgin books being buried and penetrated by worms was more than he could bear.

The librarian issued a statement. These were all books surplus to requirements.

'Notice,' said Pawley, 'she carefully doesn't even say they were duplicates. Maybe they weren't duplicates. Just surplus to requirements. It could mean anything.'

'Could be any of us,' said Dr Bee.

Another statement followed. The books were full of mildew and silverfish and posed a threat to the other holdings.

Nobody worried too much. The age of the book was passed. This was the time the university hired a public relations image team to give it market identity. They redesigned the crest. At vast expense. The logo they called it now. It used to feature an open book supported by various unlikely animals. The public relations firm deleted the book and placed the unlikely animals in politically correct embrace.

It was beyond words.

5

Cultural Studies

'I knew her when she was a research student,' said Pawley.

'Not in the Biblical sense, I hope,' said Lancaster.

'Sometimes, Henry,' said Pawley, 'your conversation is as clichéd as the dialogue of your novels.'

'Touchy today, are we?' said Lancaster. 'Dope drought again?'

'Touchy,' said Pawley, wafting off, 'touch was only a part of it. We used to call her Miss Paw Paw. In those days she was one of those people who couldn't hold a conversation without running her hands all over you.'

'I'd have thought you would have enjoyed that,' said Lancaster.

'She was always so sweaty,' said Pawley. 'Always those great damp patches at the arm pits.'

'And you prefer the fleshly parts dry, is that it?'

'Sexual harassment,' said Pawley. 'If we'd had sexual harassment legislation then, she'd have been up on a charge.'

'I thought you disapproved of sexual harassment legislation. Witch-hunting, I believe you called it,' said Lancaster.

'She was a witch,' said Pawley. 'It was a department party. She monstered me all evening. That's when we had parties in the evening, before the housekeepers found them too louche and moved them to ninety minutes at noon.'

'You seem to have found them pretty louche yourself,' said Lancaster.

'It was the way she kept on in front of my girl-friend. Plonking down on my lap. Trying to get me outside to screw her in the stairwell.'

'I gather it was the in front of your girl-friend bit you objected to,' said Lancaster, 'not the sucking out of your false-teeth in itself.'

'It was everything. She was just trouble. She was provocation. It was designed to maximise trouble. By then I'd got familiar with the strategy. I told her. I said, "You're just another fucking little secret service provocateur, so fuck off."'

'And how did she react to this elegant formulation?'

'She fucked off.'

'With anyone in particular?'

'I didn't look.'

'And your relationship blossomed ever after.'

'Absolutely,' said Pawley.

'And now she's rejoined us as a super-star, changed her sexual orientation and become our Head of Department's bosom buddy,' said Dr Bee.

But there was more to it than that, Pawley insisted.

'Whenever there's some blatant scandal, you have to look for the real manipulation beneath it. The obvious corruption is just to divert your attention from the real thing.'

'And the real thing is?' said Dr Bee.

'They needed someone to impose literary theory on us. This was the last department in the hemisphere not to have succumbed. So they rolled her in and she set up compulsory literary theory in every year.'

'She certainly did,' said Lancaster.

'It's all part of the roll back of radicalism,' said Pawley. 'They introduce this gobbledygook, promote it through the American publishers, and disempower entire generations. It's designed to block the development of a radical criticism. It diverts attention away from class and politics into form and aesthetics. Then it brings in the body and space and endless trendiness. Each year there's a new theory. It's like the motor industry of consumer capitalism. Update. Update. Compulsory pluralism. Any colour you want as long as it's black. Anything goes as long as you don't engage with social issues.'

If you looked around the other campuses you could see all the new appointments had been people who claimed a competence in theory. It was too consistent to have been mere accident. And one after another they all ran out of wind and deflated. But not before they had forced the changes on the syllabus, replaced books with the text, replaced reading the text with reading theory. Then they subsided into jellified silence, insignificant absence.

But Philippa was not narrowly theoretical. Once she had achieved the removal of books and authors from the courses she taught, she moved on pluralistically to greater opportunities. She had discovered identity, post-colonialism, cultural studies. She took leave to live with the aboriginals and took their photographs and wrote down their sacred songs.

'I swear it's all government work,' said Pawley. 'Patrol officer stuff. Find out about the black bastards to keep them down.'

She published a book. Or rather some dubious agency published it with massive taxpayer funding. *My Tribe* she called it, in the way anthropolgists used to speak of their subjects. Indifferent photographs and unreadable translations, but it made her a star. At least in her own eyes and in Germany. In Germany the New Englishes specialists embraced her. The political reaction entrenched in the German universities was such that there was little possibility of an oppositional reading of literature. So the discontented and the liberal and oppositional took the only way available - 'new' literatures as opposed to the canon. And within that category indigenous literatures were the favourite. It meant research trips to distant warm places. And they cultivated, these Germans, experts who could get them access to such places. So she was especially cultivated. She did a lot of travelling round the greater Germany, Austria, Croatia, the Sudetenland of former Czechoslovakia. It enraged Lancaster, who like to travel round those regions too. He would swan into a conference on Austral influences and find all the nubile young maidens flocking round Philippa like geese round the goose girl. And the only mädchen who spoke to him treated him with compassion.

'You do not look like we imagined you would look from your books. You look so conservative. You do not look like a writer. That tie. That jacket. Your hair so short. Are you happy with your life?'

And Lancaster, who was trying to crack the diplomatic cultural circuit by dressing like an elder of the Presbyterian church in his North American professional writer's uniform - blue blazer, grey flannels, club tie - had to stand there while the Rhine maidens stroked Philippa's anthropologists' paratrooper gear.

It seemed to Pawley that somewhere along the line the secret services recruited the brightest and the best, the schizoid and the unscrupulous, put them through some summer school course, and then planted them around the universities, the media, publishing, television and government, so that they had their people in key positions. The actual number of operatives was probably small. But these trained, recruited plants, these agents of influence, provocateurs and informers were a legion. Over the years he had refined his theories to Dr Bee and to Lancaster. He was never quite sure that Dr Bee and Lancaster weren't in that category themselves. But at least they listened. Usually people he'd tried out his theories on had pooh-poohed them, refusing to countenance any crack in the liberal veneer of the free world. But Dr Bee and Lancaster were always ready to sit around and talk, gossip, theorise and share a joint in his room. He did worry about them, he remained uncertain. But about Philippa he had no doubts at all. And now she was back from her extended leave. On staff. It could be for eternity, unless they had schemes to groom her as an ambassador to Unesco.

Dr Bee stood snuffling the air in the car park, savouring the scent of further decay and corruption. He was torn between the pleasures of contempt and the horror of perceived degradation.

Gervaise stood beside him, Breton fisherman's cap, half-spectacles chained round his neck like a row of pearls from a Bizet opera.

They were singing their duet.

'Codswallop,' Gervaise intoned.

'Pig swill,' Dr Bee wheezed in concert.

'How can any half-way civilised person put this forward as literature?' said Gervaise. He brandished a sheet of paper at Dr Bee. Philippa's outline for a post-colonial cultural studies course.

'I think you'll find literature is no longer the preferred term of reference. Literature is élitist. A more homely, housekeeperly, Germanic "writing" is the current cant. Unless you prefer "écriture."'

'Barbarism,' said Gervaise, scratching ferociously as his sea dog's beard. Most of his time he spent on his yacht. Once in a while he came ashore to pick up the *Joseph Conrad Journal* and was always appalled at the evidences of subversion, creeping socialism and tommy rot that he encountered on the mainland.

He lit up a cheroot and enveloped himself and Dr Bee in a cloud of foul smelling fumes. Dr Bee choked and moved away. He stood there irresolute, considering going back to his room to escape the fumes, when a stoned Pawley wafted up, surrounded by his own cloud of noxious vapour.

Gervaise wordlessly waved Philippa's course proposal in front of Pawley.

'Heady stuff,' said Pawley. 'Ultra-progressive.'

Gervaise growled like a sea-lion on Cannery Row.

'Don't you like it?' said Pawley. 'I'd have thought you'd have approved.'

Gervaise took a breath to deliver an outraged response and choked on his cheroot, coughing, spluttering and turning red round the edges of his beard.

'I suppose your sort of chaps think it's all jolly good,' he wheezed, his voice thinned and reduced as he struggled for air. 'Advancing the revolution and all that . . . .'

'Not at all,' said Pawley. 'Objectively counter-revolutionary. All diversion and displacement. Just another reactionary plot to block class analysis and substitute the substitute. And, of course, to discredit the very cause it claims to be advancing. It's meant to be extreme and outrageous so in the end it will provoke a backlash from people like you.'

'What people like me?' said Gervaise, his uniqueness impugned, his flag of individuality threatened with replication.

'Reactionary old shags,' said Pawley.

'Shag is what he smokes,' said Dr Bee. 'I think you meant slags.'

'I must have had some idea of self-immolation in mind,' said Pawley. 'Spontaneous combustion.'

'I've never heard such arrant nonsense,' said Gervaise.

'The proposal or the analysis?' asked Dr Bee.

'Wait till you have to teach it,' said Pawley. 'This year a special option, next year a compulsory course for every first year student.'

'The Dead Hand will never let it through,' said Gervaise.

'Want to bet on it?' said Pawley.

'We have to stand firm on this,' said Gervaise.

'That will be the day,' said Dr Bee.

Gervaise lobbied away all week, bailing up people at the bar, along the corridors, in the car park, in the gents. There was general agreement. There was always general agreement. As for Philippa, she had no need to lobby. The female faction stood solid. They would always vote as a bloc. Not that things ever came to a vote with the Dead Hand and the Head of Department. That was the one sure principle they had. Never let things come to a vote for fear people might see where potential power lay. Power lay in only one place as far as they were concerned. In their corpse-like grip.

'But where are the books, where is the literature?' asked Lancaster. 'This isn't literature. I don't mind it as sociology. Memoir. Case study. Diary writing. It is all those worthy things. Good for Sociology. Good for Ethnic Studies. But where is the literature?'

He was in his euphonic mode of expansive weariness. Weary toleration, yet warily on guard for the eternal verities. He had learned, bitterly, that confrontation achieved nothing. Certainly not confrontation with the forces of the new university. He tried acceptance now, tolerant acceptance with a plea for tolerance of the old, the true, the trusted, the valued. Tolerant questioning rather than adversarial confrontation. Not that he expected it to work.

'The future is beyond merely books,' said the Head of Department. 'The future is videos.'

'Is that a positive or a negative?' asked Dr Bee.

'Everywhere it's the same,' howled Henry. 'In the publishers' lists entertainment displaces literature. Now in the universities videos displace books.'

Pawley opposed it, but in no hopeful way.

'It'll go through,' he said. 'It's perfect. The Dead Hand will love it.'

'Love?' said Dr Bee. 'Since when do we attribute emotions to the Dead Hand?'

'He'll lap it up,' said Pawley. 'It's pure tokenism.'

'Pure?' persisted Dr Bee.

'Impure, then,' said Pawley, 'impure tokenism.'

We must be precise in our terms,' said Dr Bee.

'Pure or impure, it doesn't matter,' said Pawley, 'it's all totally phoney. It offers no threat. It's designed to block off a political analysis. It's complicit with reaction. All these pseudo courses are introduced so it looks like the university is concerned with race and minorities and so on, while at the same time any real attempts to tackle underprivilege and impoverishment and economic exploitation are dropped. At the moment equal opportunity was made official policy in the USA, funding for black educational programs was terminated. This is all part of the bullshit surface flurry designed to mask the reactionary shift of social practice. That's why the Dead Hand will accept it. He knows it's not real. The Dead Hands fought for years against any hard politics. Now they accept any ethnic, nationalist tokenism to make them seem liberal. They have to anyway. Otherwise they'd have to face anti-discrimination boards. And anti-discrimination covers race and gender, but not class and politics. All very convenient. But that's the give away. Race and gender politics were designed to displace class analysis. When I wanted to teach that course on colonialism and the novel -'

'When was that?' said Dr Bee. 'When have you ever wanted to teach any course?'

'Before I was ground down by the Dead Hand,' said Pawley, 'I wanted to teach a lot of courses. And this was one. And he tried every trick in the book to stop it. First of all he said there was no-one to back up if I got sick. He point blank refused to have it shared with History or Politics. He said if I wanted to teach it with them I could do it in my own time and it wouldn't count as one of our courses. Then he time-tabled it for two o'clock on a Friday afternoon. Then he left it out of the handbook so no one knew it was on. Then he failed to put in the text book order to the book shop. The next year he forgot to book a room.'

'But you won in the end,' said Dr Bee. 'The progressive forces of anti-colonialism won through.'

'No thanks to the Dead Hand,' said Pawley.

'The beginning of the end,' said Gervaise. 'It was people like you introducing all this cant and tommy rot who opened the floodgates to all this.'

He waved Philippa's proposal around above his head like a deranged semaphorist. 'It has to be stopped.'

'It won't be,' said Dr Bee.

Nor was it.

It was the usual meeting. Everyone ranked round the Head of Department's room with its shelves full of uninspected publishers' inspection copies.

They looked at their toes.

Philippa put forward her proposal.

Gervaise said nothing, his beard jutting out furiously but his jaw clamped tight. Pawley said nothing. How could he? Oppose racial minorities? Challenge sexual preferences? Deny populist taste, reject the video culture? It was all unassailable, unsayable.

Lancaster was in Seoul. Dr Bee never attended meetings anyway.

6

Quality Control

'Quality control,' snorted Gervaise. 'What do they think this place is?'

'We used to say it was a supermarket where students picked up items from the shelves and called it education,' said Dr Bee. 'But clearly the model is now the production line.'

'Like a bloody plastics factory,' said Gervaise. 'They'll be wanting us to put on those hair-net hats to keep our hair out of the machinery and stand along a conveyor belt next.'

Second world-war propaganda films passed before his rheumy eyes, hymns to munition factories scripted by 1930s public school poets.

'You'd look quite fetching,' said Dr Bee.

'Next they'll be asking us to clock in.'

'The electronic building-access card does that already,' said Pawley. 'Every time you use it the time and date are recorded. It registers when you come and when you go. Twenty-four hour a day surveillance.'

'None of their bloody business,' said Gervaise. 'This is supposed to be a university.'

'The life of the mind,' said Dr Bee.

'It's still better than having to work,' said Pawley. 'No heavy lifting.'

'That is the sort of attitude that has brought us to this pass,' said Gervaise.

'Which pass would that be?' Pawley asked. 'Up the Khyber Pass?'

'Are you alluding to the book or the film?' asked Dr Bee.

'Oh, the book,' said Pawley.

Gervaise stomped out.

'I'm not sure there is one,' said Dr Bee.

'Sounds convincing enough,' said Pawley. 'If there isn't one there should be. Get Henry onto the job.'

But the quality control measures were not to be disposed of. The Head of Department called a meeting.

'Accountability,' she said, 'is the new buzz-word.'

'I thought it was housekeeping,' said Lancaster.

'What is a buzz-word?' asked Gervaise.

'It's a development of the V-2 buzz-bomb,' said Pawley. 'The letter killeth. By remote control. Viral additives.'

'Accountability,' sang the Head of Department, the word music to her ears. 'As we move to taking in more fee-paying students, we have to be seen to be giving value for money.'

'It didn't matter when education was free, is that it?' said Pawley. 'But now the rich can buy an education that they were not qualified for under the old entry requirements, we have to deliver.'

'I would hope you always delivered,' said the Head of Department.

'Absolutely,' said Henry. 'We deliver.'

'The university as take-away pizzeria,' said Pawley. 'Extra pineapple for me.'

'Anchovies,' said Gervaise.

'Gentlemen,' said the Head of Department, 'when you've finished. This is a serious matter.'

'Damn right it is,' said Gervaise.

'I am proposing that we have a trial marking session to ensure our standards are consistent across the board.'

'Shouldn't we involve the enthusiastic as well as the bored?' asked Henry.

But since Dr Bee never attended meetings there was no one to ask who they might be.

Sample essays were photocopied and circulated. Staff were instructed to arrive with them marked at a meeting in the Head of Department's room. She had installed a whiteboard and when they arrived began to draw columns on it and write down their names in a row.

'Couldn't this have been done before?' Pawley muttered to Henry.

'Busy woman,' said Henry. He sat there rewriting the proofs of an interview he had given. 'She always does this,' he said. 'Puts us in our place. That's why I always bring something to work on.'

'Is that the reason?' said Gervaise. 'I thought you were just letting us know how famous you are.'

'Philippa,' the Head of Department called out, all honey and charm. 'Would you write the sample marks in the columns while I call out the names?'

'Teacher's pet,' said Gervaise.

The marks varied from nine, eleven, twelve to sixteen. Out of twenty. No one was surprised. A seven mark range on a scale of twenty was the thirty something percentage discrepancy they had learned from experience to live with, and had learned from experience not to think about, not to question, not to expose. It was when Gervaise's mark came in at eighteen that the Head of Department queried him.

'Marking them on the train as I came in this morning,' he said cheerfully. 'Must have gone through a tunnel at that point.'

'Well,' said Henry, 'that all seems very satisfactory.' He began shuffling his papers together. 'Shall we leave them with you?' he asked the Head of Department. 'Don't want confidential documents drifting round the department.'

'We're not finished yet, Henry. I have a second batch here. In order to reduce the variables, we will all mark this batch under the same conditions.'

'In Gervaise's tunnel, maybe?' asked Pawley.

'After tea we shall come back here and mark them together. We can see if marking them in this way reduces the discrepancies.'

Dr Bee was waiting for them at morning tea.

'The obvious solution,' he told them, 'is to maximise variation from each other. Otherwise she'll have us doing all our marking together. It'll be like an examination room. Forced attendance from nine to five. If you don't sabotage this now each one of us is doomed for the rest of his natural life.'

Gervaise grunted and rushed out.

They sat there speed reading and thinking of a number. When they were finished the Head of Department wiped the whiteboard and drew a new set of lines. Philippa came up marker pen in hand. The first name was called. Gervaise.

'So you can't fudge your results after you hear the rest of us,' Henry hissed at him.

‘Seventeen, twelve, fourteen, eleven, two,’ Gervaise intoned.

‘What’s this two?’ said the Head of Department. ‘There are only four papers.’

‘Five,’ said Gervaise.

‘I’ve got five,’ said Henry.

‘Me too,’ said Pawley.

‘Yes,’ the assembled staff chorused.

‘There can’t be,’ said the Head of Department. ‘There are only four.’

She walked across to Gervaise. He handed across his stack of sample papers and she flicked through them. At the fifth she went through a splendid spectrum of colour transformations. A bloodless white, a sick grey, and then a rosy red suffusion of embarrassment or rage.

‘This isn’t an essay,’ she said, ‘this is an article I am writing. Where did this come from?’

‘From the pile you gave us, my dear,’ said Gervaise.

‘I didn’t hand this out.’

‘Now you tell us,’ said Gervaise. ‘After we’ve gone and spent time marking it. Jolly embarrassing, what? If I’d known it was you I wouldn’t have given it a two. What did you give it, Henry?’

‘Oh, more than that,’ said Henry. ‘Five, I think.’

‘How about you old chap?’ Gervaise asked Pawley.

‘I think we’ll just leave this,’ said the Head of Department. ‘I find this infantile.’

‘Not infantile,’ said Gervaise. ‘A two out of twenty, immature but not infantile.’

7

Poisoned Buildings

For all the conversations, it would be wrong to give the impression that the university was a site of collegiality. Those days were gone, if they ever had been. Sometimes collegiality was invoked in opposition to the current ruling vision of managerialism. But that was just a matter of brandishing a word against a faceless force. What the word meant, what other hypocrisies it had masked or represented, were lost in the convenient mists of time.

'It used not to be as bad as this,' said Lancaster.

Dr Bee snorted, a sound from those clubman's chronicles of an earlier era, pshaw or harrumph, and took out his fob watch as an alternative to snorting up snuff. The common room stretched deolate about them, a disorder of empty chairs and worn carpet.

'It was all right till the Dead Hand's delusion of the one big building.'

To say that the Dead Hand had no ideas would be incorrect. Pawley insisted that he had no ideas about literature, or life, about art or spirit, history or love or truth. But power, power he had ideas about, power brought an electrolytic reflex into the graveyard fingers, sent a tremor down the mummified arm. Power, how to hold onto it, how to exclude others from it, was the juice that kept his system functioning. But power is abstract, hard to portray, difficult to gaze at in the miserly evenings. It is a force rather than a materiality, and his material soul wanted a material manifestation of it. That was when he conceived the idea of the Departmental building.

Until then the department was scattered. It had grown as the university had grown, and additions had been annexed and tacked on as both expanded. Some were in the original prematurely post-modern courtyard, some beneath the museum of archaeology and anthropology, some in the transient building, a forty year old ex-army temporary hut, and some in the socialist realist blocks of the fifties. It worked well. People were comparatively glad to see each other when they met. They would convene at lunch from their distant quarters. They would dissolve afterwards into their different groupings, develop separatist agendas, allow their glimmerings of individual identity to sprout like mustard and cress on a damp flannel.

The Dead Hand killed all that in one mortal stroke. In lieu of any literary ideas or educational program, he saw it as his destiny to unite the department in one Ozymandian block. His memorial monolith. Necropolis now.

The administration encouraged him. They were happy for the department to vacate the courtyard. The traditional centre of the university was no place for academics. This was the core, and the administrators were like fruit flies poised ready to occupy it.

But dreams of a new custom-built building, whatever the Dead Hand dreamed or was told, were ridiculous. No administrator would sanction a new building for the humanities. The immediate agenda was to run the humanities down, the unspoken agenda that was euphemism for the even more unspeakable agenda of running them off campus altogether, along with the pure sciences. Replace them with the applied. Applied money-making and Advanced Money-lending: Language Training for Business; Business Administration; Commerce; Tourism. The site for a new Business Studies building had already been allocated. The language laboratories were already under construction. There were new buildings for those areas.

'Here,' they said to the Dead Hand, 'how about the old Business Studies building when the Business men and women move out to their new block?' They took him round, held his icy claw and showed him the potential. He had never seen such a large professorial room as the Professor of Business Studies had. Its own toilet. An en-suite. Dream of every upward-mobile home buyer.

He bought it.

There was resistance. Lancaster said he was perfectly happy in the courtyard and refused to move. Dr Bee said he was perfectly unhappy in his bunker beneath the museum sarcophagi. But there was no solidarity. There never was, on any issue. They all moved.

The first lie was that it was the department's own building. Or the Dead Hand's. But it wasn't. They were sharing it. There were others above them and others below.

The conversion had been done in the usual university vandalistic way. Elegantly proportioned rooms partitioned into cubicles. Except for the Dead Hand's and Edwina's massive suites. The corridors were long and low and pokey, promoting unwelcome body contact, though their darkness limited offensive looking. And now people met each other continually. Thrust together, everyone realised how much they disliked each other. Herded into the one cattle pen they realised hatred was the sole emotion they held in common. The common room that in the Dead Hand's schemes could contain them all contained them all for a couple of weeks. After that people began to keep away. They came in early for tea. Or at the last minute. Shifts were established by tacit telepathy, so that they would never find themselves munching biscuits en masse. Gradually they stopped coming. And after they stopped coming to morning and afternoon tea, they stopped coming to work altogether. They appeared, presumably, for their classes, and left immediately. Within a month the building had become deserted, a morgue-like monument to the Dead Hand's long, slow, living death. Indeed, with everyone somewhere else like a European university, it began to regenerate into something almost tolerable.

'It's like one of those vast, chill country houses Evelyn Waugh used to get himself invited to to write his novels,' said Lancaster, in the echoing emptiness of the common room.

Dr Bee sniffed the air and took out his fob watch.

'Time for a spot of shooting,' he suggested.

Pawley had other theories about the conspicuous absences of his colleagues.

'They're all sick,' he said. 'It's the poisoned building syndrome. They get sick every time they come in and have to spend all their time recuperating. They probably sense it subconsciously so now they avoid coming in.'

There was plausibility to the theory. Occasionally you would catch sight of someone shuffling down a corridor in carpet slippers, mug in hand, like an inmate of a private nursing home, locked away to die.

Pawley started keeping a check of deaths in this and the adjacent buildings.

'Natural attrition,' said Lancaster. 'They're all getting on.'

'Forty-eight, fifty-five, do you call that old?' said Pawley.

'Old in spirit,' said Dr Bee.

But it was disturbing.

Then there was the very public death of one of the Asia hands in the faculty club Thanksgiving lunch queue.

'Why do we have a Thanksgiving lunch, anyway?' asked Henry. 'Are we so subservient to the USA?'

'Yes,' said Pawley.

'Are you sure it was before he'd eaten?' Dr Bee asked.

There was no doubt. One minute he was standing in the queue swapping dirty jokes with the Professor of Psychology, waiting as the turkey was carved, the next he had crashed to the ground and lay there foaming.

The Professor of Psychology called one of the medical professors over.

'Just drunk,' said the medico and turned away.

'He's not drunk, he's sick,' said the Professor of Psychology.

'With you and not drunk?' said the medico. 'Not a chance. In your company he'd be drunk just from passive drinking.'

'Do something,' said the Professor of Psychology. 'Help us.'

The Professor of Medicine put his head down and rushed out of the building.

'Probably for the best,' said one of the Professor of Psychology's drinking companions. 'Probably would have killed him if he'd tried to do anything. Hasn't handled a patient for years.'

They looked at the Asia hand lying at their feet.

Whether it was for the best or not, the Asia hand was dead anyway.

'Assassination,' said Pawley. 'All those years he spent with the hill tribes in the golden triangle growing opium for the CIA. Obviously knew too much.'

'I never saw any sign he knew anything,' said Dr Bee.

'Professional cover,' said Pawley.

'Rubbish,' said Dr Bee. 'The man was an ignorant brute.'

'Doesn't mean he wasn't a CIA asset,' said Pawley.

'Doesn't mean he wasn't an academic,' said Lancaster.

'Probably a blow dart to the neck,' said Pawley. 'Somebody in the queue behind him. One of the anthropologists.'

'Or the Professor of Medicine,' said Lancaster. 'Why did he leave so quickly?'

There were two more deaths the next day. These were laboratory technicians and a post-mortem found they died from an unknown lethal virus. After the fourth death it was announced that it was a genetically engineered virus that had escaped from the biochemistry laboratory and spread through the air-conditioning system into other departments.

'Same thing happened ten years ago, killed a couple of cleaners,' said Dr Bee. 'The department was supposed to fix up the ventilation system so it wouldn't happen again but they clearly never got around to it.'

Then the Professor of Genetic Engineering was found dead in his laboratory, with a letter addressed to the Vice-Chancellor taking full responsibility.

'In his laboratory? said Pawley. 'When did he ever go to his laboratory? Those people have research assistants to do all the laboratory work.'

'You'd have thought he would have chosen a bath and done it in the Roman way,' said Dr Bee. 'No sense of style or tradition, these people.'

'The report says natural causes,' said Lancaster.

Dr Bee and Pawley laughed wearily in unison.

'It's obvious they held a gun to his head and made him make the confession,' said Pawley. 'Then shot him up with some non-traceable lethal substance.'

'And why would they do that?'

'Silence him,' said Pawley. 'Make it look like an error he was taking responsibility for. Obviously it was a deliberate field test. They always use air-conditioning systems. Practice for feeding stuff into foreign embassies. Remember legionnaire's disease? That came through the air-conditioning. Obvious they used the gathering of legionnaires to practice on. They used to use soldiers or prisoners in the past. Now there are more controls on what they can do in prisons and army camps so they've turned to campuses.'

'I thought your previous theory was they'd assassinated the Asia hand.'

'Could've done. Used the virus on him and bumped off the Professor of Genetic Engineering to keep it quiet.'

'Actually,' said Lancaster, 'I must confess I do find it a more comforting scenario than the alternative. At least this suggests some conscious intent. Otherwise you have to postulate uncontrolled lethal virus experiments taking place on campus with no controls, and the viruses escaping up the ventilation shafts and out the doors through sheer academic incompetence. I find that even more frightening.'

'The truth generally is frightening,' said Dr Bee.

The deaths continued over the years. Less dramatically. Natural wastage perhaps. But Pawley kept his file on them. Too many tumours, too many cancers.

'It's either viruses they keep on testing, or selective assassination.'

'Oh yes?' said Dr Bee. 'Who would want to assassinate the walking dead?'

'They're still targeting the left,' Pawley insisted. 'Still bumping off anyone who speaks out.'

'Who speaks out?' said Dr Bee.

'Exactly. There's no one any more. They've all died or been invalided out.'

'But the deaths go on? Who are the victims now?'

'Ex-agents,' said Pawley confidently. 'Secret service spooks they fixed up with jobs in Politics and Asian Studies and English and Anthropology. They did their tour of duty, their cover got blown, so they retired them here. Some are dying of cancer from radiation exposure in the course of their jobs. Others they've decided are insecure so they're terminating them.'

'Henry,' said Dr Bee. 'You should use some of the products of Pawley's florid imagination for your fiction.'

But Lancaster was preoccupied in reading about the possible side-effects of the latest medication his doctor had prescribed him for one of his undiagnosable sicknesses.

Meanwhile the Dead Hand and Deadwood Edwina and the Head of Department continued unaffected.

Like cockroaches they seemed to be of a different biology, not requiring oxygen, not susceptible to any of the diseases of mortal life.

8

Department Library

When Edwina was elevated to Pro-Vice-Chancellor, she looked round her former professorial room with a tortured moment of regret. So large a room. So magnificent a fireplace. Such marvellously mullioned windows. It was far too good for anyone else to occupy. She savoured this exquisite moment of farewell. Après moi le deluge. The tears poured out and were rapidly retracted. No one should have it. There should be no inheritance. It should be a memorial, a shrine, a veritable necropolis.

Her slightly salty eyes swept around the bookshelves, the elegant timber shelves she had insisted on, refusing the regulation grey steel issue. The spines of the books stared back at her glumly, stacked in there and never taken out for exercise, dead men and women's brains, ranked like skulls in the catacombs. They exuded silent, sullen recrimination for what she had never read, for what she had never written.

She shuddered. She found them distasteful. Dusty, musty,

fusty. Was fusty a word? She looked at the serried ranks of the *Oxford English Dictionary on Historical Principles.* She would dirty her hands if she took it out to consult. First thing she would do as PVC would be to order it on CD-Rom so her secretary could key it up for her.

Light broke in from the east. The room was illuminated in a glow of perception. She would be an all-electronic PVC. Maybe the first all-electronic PVC. Not a book should sully her shelves. The paper-free office. Except the en-suite of course. She didn't want some electronic mouse wiping her arse. Might need paper there. Though there was always the possibility of a bidet. Why not? She would be a thoroughly modern PVC. And the books. The room throbbed with the vision of it. She would bequeath the books to the Department. This should be the beginnings of a departmental library.

They had never had a departmental library. Indeed she had resolutely opposed one every time they idea had been raised. But now was the time. It would save moving the wretched things. She could arrange a tax credit for the gift which, given the tax rate on a PVC's salary, would be worth far more than she could ever get by trying to sell them to a second-hand dealer. And she would be rid of them. They depressed her. It was like going to the library, all those books people had written, including people she had known, she found it all infinitely depressing. Menacing. Threatening. Now they could menace other people. And that way no one would ever have the room after her. It would remain in memory hers eternally. And as a library it would for ever be still and empty. No one in a department of literature would ever use a library. Those who wanted them had their own books, those few. The others would never go near it. It would rest in the immemorial silence of a Pharaoh's tomb. For ever unpenetrated. And a mummy's curse on those who dared to enter in.

She stood there, Edwina, in the huge arena, lost in the magnificence of it, but smiling, smiling, what a stroke of genius.

She announced the proposal at a departmental meeting. Who could oppose it? Edwina's gift. How could they refuse to inherit her library?

'Every volume untouched by human hand,' said Dr Bee.

The decision was made, ratified, finalised. That was it.

And once a PVC, Edwina ensured that her chair should be no more. The faculty was in financial difficulties. What was needed were career opportunities for young staff. Young women. You could have three young women on contract for the price of one professor. The way forward was young women on contract. The university was committed to equal opportunity. As it proclaimed at the bottom of all its job advertisements, the University is a non-smoking workplace and is committed to the policies and principles of equal opportunity and cultural diversity and public transport for non-administrative staff. How could it claim that and not appoint more young women? Particularly on contract. The Ministry was committed to removing tenure. How could they appoint more tenured professors? So the deed was done. The chair disestablished, abolished. Edwina had been the last of her line. And her room remained her silent memorial.

It never proved possible to establish the library. Henry had the bright idea of supplementing Edwina's gift. He assembled a complete collection of his own works, variant editions, volumes in translation. He could see his own memorial there, a little urn within the necropolis. The Lancaster library. But the Head of Department refused.

'We can't take in more books until we have had a surveyors' report,' she said. 'The university architect has advised we need to get the floor strengthened if it is to be a library.'

'Prolific as I am held to be,' said Henry, with what he could summon up for modesty, 'I hardly think my collected works are so heavy as to collapse the floor.'

'It's the principle of the thing,' said the Head of Department. 'If we put yours in then other people may offer the same.'

'With due respect,' said Henry, 'even if we included the entire department's publication output in quadruplicate, it is not going weigh more than the standard airline baggage allowance.'

'They may want to follow Edwina's example,' said the Head of Department.

Henry held back from speculating which example.

'And donate some of their personal library.'

'Throw their books out you mean,' he said.

'It could well mean some considerable accessions.'

'Well, move the library to somewhere with a stronger floor and I'll take the room,' offered Henry.

'No, we can't do that, the room has been designated already.'

'Designated as what?'

'Designated as not a private office.'

And even with the books that were there, there was no librarian to check them in and out, so it was never possible to use them.

'The books will be stolen unless we have a librarian,' said the Head of Department.

'There's nothing worth stealing,' said Dr Bee.

'On the contrary, it is an extremely valuable collection.'

'So valuable we deny everyone access to it,' said Pawley.

'Have you ever heard of anyone stealing books in this place?' asked Dr Bee. 'Except for Henry stealing back his own signed copies when he thought they weren't being appreciated by whoever he gave them to.'

But what could they do? Roster academics to library duty? Not a chance. Have an honour system for borrowing? That was universally dismissed. No one had any illusions that there was any honour in the department. Conscript senior students? Again, that was rejected, there was no honour among students either, and no one wanted to deal with them, not since the new sexual harassment guidelines.

So the room remained empty, the books no more disused than when Edwina had inhabited, the light coming and going as day succeeded night, the silence settling there, spelling out the end of the age of literacy to absent ears.

9

Social Call

Henry was leafing through misfiled papers when someone knocked.

'Come in,' he shouted out, so they'd hear the other side of the door, so he didn't have to move across and open it, carrying on shuffling through the folders.

'Yes,' he said.

'Yes sir, excuse me, Professor Lancaster, sir, I'm an American graduate student,' the visitor began, 'and I'd like to do some graduate work on the political novel.'

Henry emitted a spontaneous howl of horror.

'Have you spoken to the person in charge of graduate studies?' he said, keeping his head down as he carried on shuffling through his papers, academic origami they called it.

'Not exactly.'

'That's your first step,' said Henry.

There was no sound of departure. He shuffled a bit more but nothing happened. Finally Henry looked up. It wasn't going to go away. If it was a hallucination it was clearly here to stay. Reality is a hallucination, as Pawley never tired of saying.

'I was only kidding,' the visitor said. 'You probably don't remember me,' he went on. 'Cannon's the name.'

'Cannon !' boomed Henry. He thought he did it very well. In these days of self analysis, of close scrutiny of one's own reactions, he was always ready to allow himself some praise, some recognition that once in a while he didn't fuck up. He hadn't said, 'Not another bloody American,' or 'Yankee go home,' or indeed anything awful. He'd managed not to say anything very much at all, in fact. He'd played it by the rules and it seemed to have worked. He must try that more often, he figured. He even remembered Cannon now. And the thesis on the political novel.

'It's been a long time,' said Henry.

'It certainly has,' said Cannon. 'I thought I was going to get bawled out for suggesting supervision.'

Henry made clucking noises he'd learned over in England. He felt they'd be more appropriate than saying, Could have.

'So what have you been up to?' he asked.'Oh, a bit of this and a bit of that,' Cannon said. 'I was on a tugboat in Vietnam. Then I was in the Middle East a while. Then I taught college. Now I'm in books.'

'Books?' said Henry. 'That's nice.'

He smiled welcomingly.

'Yeah, educational publishing. Let me give you my card.'

International Division, it read.

'So I thought I'd drop by and present you with a few desk copies.'

'That's very nice of you,' Henry said.

'You'd like some?' said Cannon. 'Books? Really? I'll send you some. I was only kidding. I'm out looking over our operation here. I don't do too much leg work these days. But I'm sure I can find you some books. Let me know what you want. I'll mail you a catalogue. I'm on my way across to a session at your American Center. So I figured I should look up a few old friends while I was here. You know, just drop by, see if you were up to the same old tricks, make sure nothing's changed.'

'Iran, oh yes,' Cannon said, 'I was there. I was in a car attacked by these Iranian hoodlums. We were stuck in this traffic jam. Teaching English. I worked for an electronics company and they'd sold all this equipment to the Shah. And it wasn't light-bulbs and adaptor plugs, let me tell you. Multi-multi-multi-million dollar business. And it involved a service contract. Teaching these Iranian military personnel English. Our company had evolved a program and we were locked up in some little place in Vermont learning all this teaching package, neat system, all labelled top secret, bullshit it was, it was all there in *Janes' Aircraft* and *Aviation Week*.

'So we were out there when it all collapsed. All these shells flying across the airstrip. We worked from this hangar at the airfield. So our boss finally calls it a day and we quit teaching and head off home and get caught in this traffic jam. And this mob of Iranians starts rocking the car. So I say to the girl with me, I suggest you take a deep and serious review of your life because within about a minute they're going to pull us out of the car and stomp me to death and rape you and stomp you to death and then burn us, unless we catch fire earlier if they try to roll the car over so I'd switch off the ignition with that latter eventuality in mind. And for that minute we faced the stark reality of death.'

'But you survived, clearly,' said Henry.

'They saw some gas station being looted so they ran across there and joined in. All the foreign gas stations, airlines, and banks were attacked all over town. Don't tell me that was spontaneous. So they went. And the car to our right edged forward a few feet and I said, right, let's get out of here and go so we sort of literally forced our way through this solid mass of cars, bruised a few fenders, and then across a couple of vacant blocks and into a side street and then back to her apartment, she lived in the Armenian quarter, and sat on the rooftop watching Teheran burn. Well, it seemed like it was burning, there were fires from these looted buildings burning everywhere, every suburb.'

'Exciting times,' said Henry.

'Well, in the words of the poet, that's showbusiness,' said Cannon.

'Clearly,' said Henry.

'Talking of poetry,' said Cannon, 'are you still teaching your Masters of Modernism course?'

'I don't remember that.'

'I do,' said Cannon. 'Never forgotten it. Imprinted on the memory. All these young students coming in expecting Wallace Stevens and Allen Ginsberg and what do they get? Ho Chi Minh and Mao.'

'Oh that,' said Henry. 'That was a long time ago. It would have to be Mistresses of Modernism now.'

'It's within living memory,' said Cannon. 'There's still kids walking around out there who were influenced by it.'

'There were other texts on the course as well,' said Henry.

'Sure,' said Cannon. 'Faiz, Hikmet, MacDiarmid, Neruda, Ritsos. See, I never forget a name. What a Commie line up. Amazing they let you get away with it. Now if you'd been in the States. . . .'

'What if you'd been in the States?' asked Pawley.

'He just tailed off,' said Henry. 'Left it unsaid.'

'Unusual for an American,' said Dr Bee.

'Not even information gathering,' said Pawley, 'just issuing menaces. The unsaid's always the worst. Leaves it to the imagination. Never fails.'

'He just got up and started looking along the bookshelves,' said Henry.

'Very menacing,' said Pawley. 'I warned you about having all those volumes of Mao and Marx on show. You should have hidden them.'

'Burned them,' said Dr Bee. 'Had a bonfire in the library forecourt as an act of public contrition. "I recant." Rehabilitated yourself.'

'Otherwise it looks like you still believe in it,' said Pawley.

Henry bristled. 'Of course –,' he began.

'There you are,' said Pawley. 'I suppose you gave the same assurances to your American friend. Even as we speak the word flies across the Pacific. All ports alert, Henry Lancaster, unregenerate fellow-traveller, detain on entry.'

Henry sat there in ashen mode.

'He's just a former graduate student,' he said.

'Of course,' said Pawley. 'So are they all.'

'What do you mean?'

'That's their recruitment requirement.'

Henry grunted.

'And watch out,' Pawley added. 'They always come in threes in my observation.'

'Not single spies but in battalions,' said Dr Bee.

'Who was that female person I saw coming out of your room? Are you sure about her?' Pawley asked.

'Cannon was out here on business. He was just paying a social call,' said Henry.

'That's right,' said Dr Bee. 'You keep telling yourself that and it won't come true.'

'What won't come true?' said Henry.

'What you know,' said Dr Bee, 'the worst thing that could ever happen to you, precisely what you fear.'

10

In the Lists

It was list time. It was always list time, these times. Activities report. Research report. Publications report. University report. Faculty review. Departmental review. Personal development review. CV update. Review of reviews. Health questionnaire. Physical activity questionnaire. List of graduates supervised. Every other week there was another list to complete.

Dr Bee stood beside the paper recycling bag, opening his mail over it and dropping it in after a cursory glance.

'The business of the university,' said Pawley. 'Compiling lists and filling in forms.'

'It's an utter nonsense,' said Lancaster. 'What ever happens to them when you've filled them in?'

'If you fill them in,' said Dr Bee, dropping yet another request for information into the recycling bag.

'Clearly no one looks at them because they keep on asking for the same things,' said Lancaster.

'That's to correlate your replies,' said Pawley. 'That's how they check if you're lying.'

'What?' said Lancaster.

'They key all the data into the computers and the computers are programmed for discrepancies. Like social services computers. That's how they catch you out. Like the tax department. You claim depreciation on your library and say it's worth $60,000. Next year you forget what you said and make up another figure, $100,00. So they come and audit you.'

'Do you mean to tell me all these piddling reports are being processed and collated somewhere?'

'Of course,' said Pawley. 'Why do you think they want them?'

'Just to make us wretched,' said Lancaster. 'Just to waste our time and stop us getting on with any real work.'

'Well there is that,' Pawley agreed. 'But they figure someone will figure that out anyway. That's just the distraction. Beneath that there's the hidden reason of data collection.'

'I'd have thought that was the perfectly explicit reason,' said Dr Bee.

'Well it is, of course,' said Pawley. 'But they assume nobody takes anything at face value so no one will think it really is serious data collection. They figure people will look for the hidden reason - general time-wasting and destabilising. But beneath that is the hidden reason.'

'The surface reason,' said Dr Bee.

'Well, yes and no,' said Pawley.

'As far as I'm concerned it's all a damn waste of time and paper,' said Lancaster.

'That's what most people thought and that's why people didn't bother filling them in.'

'Indeed,' said Dr Bee.

'So when the report was leaked to the media, that's why we got such a bad press.'

'What report?' said Lancaster. 'I never saw any report.'

'You were probably out of the country,' said Dr Bee. 'Waving to your friends across the demilitarised zone.'

'The report said the average academic in the humanities published one article and gave one conference paper every five years.'

'Sounds a bit rigorous,' said Dr Bee.

'It's all used to cut funding to the humanities,' said Pawley. 'Makes us look idle.'

'We are idle,' said Dr Bee.

'Speak for yourself,' said Lancaster. 'Personally I make a point of publishing any conference paper I give as an article later.'

'Under a different title, of course,' said Dr Bee. 'So you get two for the price of one. Write one, get one free.'

'Of course,' said Lancaster. 'No one ever reads anything you do. They just read these damn lists, if they ever read them.'

'They don't read them,' said Pawley. 'They scan them electronically. Looking for correlations and discrepancies. Checking if you forgot to change the title sufficiently and were counting the same piece twice. The Ministry found there was a forty-eight per cent error in the reporting of academic publications. People putting things in the wrong categories. Claiming five page articles as books. Listing the same paper twice under different names. Forty-eight per cent error sounds high for mere error, wouldn't you think? Sounds like downright dishonesty to me. Apart from that they check to see who's inviting who to write for what. Ah, here's old Henry Lancaster in this book edited by that old commo fellow-traveller, fancy that.'

Lancaster blenched. 'How did you know about that?'

'Stab in the dark, actually,' grinned Pawley.

'One man's stab in the dark is another man's stab in the back,' said Dr Bee. Enigmatically. At least that was how Lancaster took it. Enigmatically.

And then the rules changed. Maybe the Ministry was having trouble collecting the data. Too many people throwing the forms away. Or not filling them in fully. So they introduced a cash incentive. Instead of research funds being distributed to the department on the basis of each department's publication record, now it was distributed to each individual. The more you published, the more you got. And not just publications. Grants too. You listed any research grant you had received and you were scored for that too. The bigger the grant, the bigger the score, and the more money you got. You didn't even have to publish anything, just apply for a research grant. Just writing a grant application was scored as the equivalent of publishing an article, whether you got the grant or not. Anything you might ever have thought of, you applied for a research grant to research.

It was a simple incentive but it worked. Individual greed.

'It's a travesty of intellectual life,' Lancaster fumed.

'That's our business,' beamed Pawley. 'That is what we are on this earth to do. Travesty.'

'Look at this,' said Lancaster. 'Just look at the way they think. They make you list journal articles first, books second. Isn't a book a greater achievement than a piddling journal article?'

'For a man who's written twenty-three volumes, the answer must surely be yes.'

'Thirty-three if you count the edited ones.'

'But of course,' said Pawley. 'He said he was the editor of a famous edited book.'

Lancaster glowered. 'We're run by scientists and philistines. Just because they never write a book they have to downgrade books. Just because all they produce are piddling two page articles with fifteen co-authors and written by their graduate students, they have to impose their model on all of us. How can I fill in a form like this?'

'Don't,' said Dr Bee.

'You're not going to?'

'Why should I prop up the Dead Hand? If he wants to claim this department is an intellectual hot spot, let him write something himself for once. I don't propose to give him any support.'

'So you're not filling the form in?'

'I've thrown it away,' said Dr Bee. 'How can I fill it in?'

'But I need to,' said Lancaster. 'I need the research score. I need the research funds it gives me.'

'The Bulgarians no longer offering free trips?' said Dr Bee.

Lancaster sat at his desk. When he wasn't writing fiction there was nothing he liked better than to work on his curriculum vitae. He pressed the computer keys with eager delight, opened the folder on himself, HENRY LANCASTER, opened up the CV file, scrolled through to the publications. And there it all was, his life's work, every novel, every story, every magazine excerpt, every translation. The mail would arrive with a serious looking journal in some language he couldn't read, often in a script he couldn't read, maybe with a covering note from the translator indicating what it was that was translated. And with what delight he would add it into the CV, yet another airing for a story written twenty ears ago, now in Punjabi, now in Slovenian, and he would meticulously key in the journal, the anthology, the date, the page numbers, the translator's name, the translation of the journal's name, place of publication, it was a work of art in itself the publication list, the list of all his writings.

It was a work of bejewelled exotica, from the plains of Hungary to the plains of Uzbekistan, from the paddy fields of Bengal to the paddy fields of Esarn, a glowing library of Alexandria, a humming tower of Babel, a library of continual congress.

He sat at it extracting the year's work. For further sensual delight he had taken the assorted publications from his shelves. The floor was covered with issues of *Knjizevna rec* (Beograd), *The Literary Criterion* (Mysore), *Nagy Vilag* (Budapest), *World Literature* (Beijing), *Gargoyle* (Washington, DC). Undervalued at home but what a fame abroad. He leaned back and shone in the glow of his reflected image.

But Pawley had intruded doubts. Pestilential Pawley, the unreconstructed, seventies, dope-smoking Pawley, Pawley the for ever stoned, saturated with molecules of THC, permeated with theories of the CIA, an unregenerate, still-walking psylocibin vision of conspiracy and paranoia.

He picked up *Srpski knjizevni glasnik,* the *Serbian Literary Herald.* Was it such a good idea to list it? And the others. *Gradina, Most, Politika.* Would this be seen as trading with the enemy? Every government did it. But he wasn't government. What if some over-zealous analyst up at the Ministry noticed and passed the information along to ASIO. MI6. CIA. MOSSAD. He was getting as mad as Pawley. He was infected by Pawley's craziness. He must have inhaled some of Pawley's permanent aura.

But it made such a good list. Twelve stories in Serbian translation. Another three in Chinese. And Bengali, what about Bengal, so it was a communist regime, did it matter, would anyone register, two novels in Bengali, how could he not list them?

What a jewelled list it was. How impoverished it would be without this exotica.

Dr Bee came in. The imperatives of lunch time.

'Do you think that freak Pawley was talking sense?' Lancaster asked.

'Depends what he'd been ingesting into his system,' said Dr Bee.

'About the publication report form.'

'I threw it away.'

'That's because you never publish,' said Lancaster.

Dr Bee shot one of his vicious looks but Lancaster was oblivious, lost in his own agonies.

'I'm wondering if he was right. I'm not sure about listing all this Serbian stuff.'

'What stuff is this?'

'Translations of stories. Should I include them in the report?'

'As I recall,' recalled Dr Bee, 'for years you endlessly complained that the Dead Hand always left your fiction off the publication list.'

'He did, the bastard,' said Lancaster. 'Every year I'd give him a list of everything I'd published and every year he'd edit out the fiction.'

'And now you're proposing to do the same.'

'Well, not exactly. Well, not quite. Well, yes, I suppose I am.'

'Maybe he had a point.'

'I find that hard to believe.'

'Self-censorship rather than burning by the inquisition.'

'Well, yes. I mean, if there is an inquisition, why give them fuel for the flames?'

'Why indeed.'

'Is there, do you think?'

'Is there what?'

'An inquisition.'

'Only one way to find out.'

'What's that?'

He gestured at the journals strewn over the floor. 'List all these.'

Lancaster tapped on Pawley's door. There was the sound of drawers opening and shutting, rustlings, movements. Pretty well everyone else in the department kept their doors open when they were in. To show they were there. To show no sexual congress with students was taking place. But Pawley's door was resolutely shut. Lancaster tried the handle. Locked.

Pawley let him in. The windows were wide open. The fan was on. But the room still reeked of dope. Pawley blinked at him, eyes bright pupils of blue amidst bloodshot irises.

He pressed the lock button on the door again and sat down at his desk. Lancaster took a chair. No point waiting to be asked. Unlike Lancaster's computer, glowing with cosmopolitan data, Pawley's was blank, closed down. He opened a drawer and took out his plastic bag of marijuana and began to roll a joint. A three paper one for visitors. Lancaster knew there was no point in beginning until the ritual was completed. Pawley lit up, took two or three deep drags and passed the joint across. Lancaster took a drag, and then brought up the subject of the publications list.

'What do you think they would do?'

'If you listed all those dodgy places you publish in?'

'They're not really dodgy.'

'Well, they're either under United Nations sanctions or under communist governments or anti-American regimes.'

'Well, what would they do?'

'Oh, block research grants. Intervene in promotion committees. Tip off passport control. Alert international publishers so you don't sell foreign rights in the free world. Let your tyres down. Kill your dog. Those sorts of things.'

Lancaster was visibly shaken. As the day wore on the horror of it all had seized him, exacerbated now by the paranoid potentiating qualities of the dope. Pawley passed the joint across again. Lancaster refused.

'Go on,' said Pawley. 'Steady your nerves. You look worried.'

'Well it is worrying,' said Lancaster petulantly.

'You don't have to list everything. Just forget to put them down.'

'It's not that,' said Lancaster. 'Or not only that. It's the money.'

Pawley took the joint back and grinned.

'What do you need it for? To publish more books to score more research funds to publish more books?'

'Yes,' said Lancaster.

'I rest my case,' said Pawley. 'Hooked.'

'It adds up to quite a lot,' said Lancaster. 'Every story counts.'

'Under the shadow in the dale, every shepherd tells his tale,' said Pawley.

'I could use that money.'

'What for?'

'Well, practically anything. You've seen the research protocols.'

'Not exactly,' said Pawley.

'You must have,' said Lancaster. 'It was that desperate memo saying spend all your research funds by October, otherwise they'll all be clawed back to general revenue. They drew up a list of how you could spend it for those too stupid to think for themselves. Now it's all down on paper. Anything goes. Everything's legitimised. You must have seen it.'

'Can't say I have,' said Pawley, rolling another.

'It was circulated.'

'I'm sure,' said Pawley. 'I can't read everything that's circulated. As Dr Leavis said about reading *Tom Jones,* Life's too short. I'd rather read *Tom Jones*.'

'You'd rather smoke your life away.'

'As a matter of fact,' he said, 'cannabis extends time. You end up living more, not less.'

He offered the joint again. Lancaster took it without demur.

'You haven't said what you want the funds for.'

'Anything,' said Lancaster. 'You can use them for anything. Travel. Accommodation. Books. You can just buy books. Conferences. Teaching relief.'

'Teaching relief?' said Pawley. 'What's that?'

'You pay someone to do your teaching for you while you're busy doing research.'

'Really?' said Pawley. 'Sounds a ripper. What research do you have to do?'

'Whatever you like. No one looks at it, you know that.'

'Sounds perfect,' said Pawley.

'I know,' said Lancaster. 'That's why I was going to list as much as I could. The more you list, the more you get.'

'That's what I mean,' said Pawley. 'It's a perfect sting for self-incrimination. It capitalises on every academic's petit-bourgeois greed and competitiveness. For a piddling amount of cash and to prove you've published more than your colleagues you end up listing every fragment you can think of. There it all is, down on file. And the stasi don't even have to raise a finger. You do it all for them. It's the most thorough scoop-up of data in history, all motivated by greed and competition. The twin motors of our capitalist ideology. And when they've collected all the data for five years they'll change the rules. They'll set up some research institute and give it all the money and you won't be able to claim any for yourself. But everything you ever did will be down on file. For ever after. You'll see.'

Lancaster pondered on that.

'You might have a point,' he conceded.

Pawley grinned his yellow toothed smile. The wisps of smoke hung beneath the ceiling. Time extended.

'Are you,' said Lancaster, 'are you going to roll another?'

'For you,' said Pawley, 'anything is possible.'

He reflectively licked the papers, began assembling the joint.

'So I'd best not fill in everything,' Lancaster said. Reflectively. Sadly but reflectively.

'Probably too late,' said Pawley. 'The central data registry is programmed for discrepancy. It'll be picked up. "Ah, what's happened to Henry Lancaster, suddenly there are no more translations of his work in Cuba or Serbia or China. No record of any change of heart in the old bugger. Must be concealing something. Better do a break-in of his office, see what's he's hiding. Punch up the Security Council listing of the contents of hostile nations' literary journals, see what he's been publishing that he won't tell us about."'

'I don't believe it,' said Lancaster.

'Feel free,' said Pawley. 'It's a free world, after all.'

'Absolutely,' said Lancaster.

'How do you think the free world won and the Soviet Union lost? By being freer? Or by having a more efficient state security system?'

'Stop it,' said Lancaster.

'Why do you think they try and get us to fill in these forms all the time? Why is it all centralised now? Now the universities have no independent research funds. Now it's all controlled from the capital. Why? For efficiency? Clearly not. It's just another additional bureaucracy. Why then? Just for bureaucracy's sake?'

'Yes,' said Lancaster.

'That's what they want you to think. Everyone takes the boring old intellectual liberal line and laughs at bureaucrats. Everyone thinks it's a joke - forms, forms, forms, lists, lists, lists. But that's just to wear you down. Stop you being alert. Because it's all being recorded and correlated. Now they want a profile not just of every university but of every university department. And not just of every department but of every academic employed. Now why would the Ministry want that? A file on every individual academic. This is like the centralisation that destroyed eastern Europe. Now we've taken it on over here.'

'I thought you claimed the West destroyed Eastern Europe,' said Lancaster.

'But all those centralised state controls we all inveighed against . . . .'

'I never heard you inveigh against them.'

'Well, anyway,' said Pawley, 'now we have them here.'

'It's the same with all those biographical dictionaries,' Pawley went on, the afternoon sun adding to the gentle glow, colouring the clouds of smoke with a soft golden tinge.

'What biographical dictionaries?'

'All those Who's Who of Poets and Novelists you're always filling in forms for. Dictionaries of Famous Fictioneers.'

'Which ones?'

'Any of them. They all seem suspect to me.'

'How do you know? You think everything's suspect.'

'I don't know,' said Pawley, 'nobody ever knows for sure. But if I was running the secret services, I'd certainly set up something like them. Who wants them? What use are they?'

'Well,' Lancaster bridled, 'someone might want to look me up.'

'Who would want to look you up, Henry, except the secret services? Some female fan? Some Japanese geisha? You've impaled yourself on your vanity again. Wow, look, here am I invited to be in an International Directory of Global Novelists. Fame, glory. List your hobbies - fellow-travelling. Clubs - Writers for Freedom, Novelists against Capital. Editorial positions - advisory board, *Liberation Literature, Working Papers in Class, Culture and Communism.* Visiting lectureships - Cuba, North Korea. . . . They scoop it all up, books, journals contributed to, date of birth, education, school, university. Then they can correlate you with all their data banks. Who was at university at the same time, what defector, which double-agent, what unsound chaps and chapesses you were up with, fascinating. And then they do your astrological chart from the dates you give them - easy enough, all computerised - and they can analyse all your personality traits, all your susceptibilities, how to ensnare you - greed, competitiveness, vanity, insecurity.'

'I'm not sure about insecurity,' Lancaster said.

The room shimmered gently.

No, he couldn't deny it. His novelist's imagination could believe it all too easily.

'Even that bit where it says list other writers you'd recommend for inclusion. Well, it's a long shot, most writers are too competitive and individualist to give a mention of any others. But your temporarily closest friends, you might recommend them. And there you are. They've got your associates on record. They know everything about you. And what they don't know, they know where to look to find out.'

Dr Bee was waiting for them at afternoon tea.

'Happy form filling?'

Lancaster just grunted. He steered uncertainly over to the table, tea cup shaking in its saucer, stoned, shattered.

'Cull out all the incriminating ones?'

Lancaster gave another grunt.

'What about the Muslim fundamentalists?'

'What about them?'

'I thought you had an Iranian translator. Isn't that a bit tricky too?'

'How did you know about that?'

'The administrative officer showed me the lovely Iranian stamps you gave her for her charity collection.'

Lancaster grunted again.

'She said she's asked you to give her whole envelopes since they're more valuable like that, but you didn't seem to want to. Worried about your name being bandied around with exotic stamps beside it?'

Lancaster sipped at his tea.

'You're spilling it,' said Dr Bee. 'Do you want me to get you a straw?'

'Fuck off,' said Lancaster.

'Ah, the novelist speaks. How would they translate that into

Urdu?'

'They're not.'

'Really? So what happened to your translations?'

'They never came out.'

'You're very laconic.'

'The guy's house burned down.'

It was Dr Bee's turn to spill his tea. He tried to suppress his laugh. It seemed like bad form to laugh at personal tragedy.

'You think you jinxed him?'

'I don't even want to consider the possibilities.'

'You think the fundamentalists discovered he was receiving parcels of Western decadence? Was it your novels or your parlour pink lit. crit?'

'I refuse to think about it.'

'Maybe the SAS sent in an arson squad to stop the spread of Henry Lancaster,' Pawley suggested.

Lancaster sat silent, spreading nothing.

'Maybe,' said Dr Bee, 'you should consider burning some of your books yourself. I mean, not listing them on the data base is one thing. But what if someone casts an eye along your shelves? Some innocent seeming student who's been recruited? That American graduate student you used to supervise who called the other day? Much better to do it yourself than be burned in person. Fulke Greville did it. Burned his manuscripts. Mind you it still didn't save him from being murdered while he was having a shit. But then you don't have a manservant you're having an affair with. Do you?'

'I have to go,' said Lancaster. He got up.

Dr Bee reached into his pocket.

'Box of matches, if you want them,' he offered.

11

Sacrificing the Scapegoat

Robert's problem, or one of his problems, was thelecture. It was an excruciating torture. For him, for his audience. He was seized by terror. He would stand thereunable to begin, frozen, the words piled up behind an immovable barrier.

'It's the German academic hour,' said Lancaster. 'All lectures time-tabled for the hour start at fifteen minutes past.'

So for fifteen minutes the students would sit there as Robert approached the lectern, veered away, coughed, turned to the board, wiped off the detritus of the previous class, dropped the board duster once, twice, three times. But even the three-fold thumping on the floor, the epic proclamation, the knocking at the gate, was not enough to get him started. Sometimes he almost got there, a word almost emerged, and then a late-comer would crash through the door, sucking up soft drink through a straw or chewing on a sandwich, and Robert would be thrown again, wait till the student was settled down, prepare an utterance, and another would saunter in, or a couple wrapped in each others' arms, and again the words would retreat.

Even when he got going it was a painful torrent of uncertainty, tentative expression retracted and cancelled, self-deprecating chuckles, asides, modifiers, as it weres.

Yet on stage, in the department play, he was confident and charismatic, Henry V, Hamlet, Lear, Lady Bracknell, Winnie the Pooh, he could do them all.

'Why don't you just act your lectures?' asked Dr Bee. 'Treat them like a script by somebody else and deliver them like a play?'

'Oh, I couldn't do that,' said Robert. 'Oh no, that wouldn't be right, that wouldn't be, you know -'

'No, I don't know,' said Dr Bee.

'Sincere. Authentic. Honest.' He fumbled his way through the thesaurus.

It was Dr Bee's turn to be struck dumb. It had never entered his head that those terms had anything to do with it. He still doubted that they did. But he was frozen speechless at Robert's high morality.

That was another of Robert's qualities. His infectiousness. Not in the high moral area. That was something that could not survive in the atmosphere. Once out of the host organism it rapidly withered in an academic environment. Maybe it needed direct consciousness transmission. But other things he transmitted all too well.

'I saw him walking across the campus on the way in,' said Lancaster. 'He was grinning away to himself, laughing and chuckling as he walked through the courtyard, oblivious of everything. I couldn't help laughing. And then I realised people were looking at me strangely. There I was. Doing the same thing. Laughing and grinning to myself. The man's a menace.'

He started again, chuckling as he remembered it, his teacup shaking in his saucer.

Dr Bee eyed him doubtfully.

'I'd get a check up if I were you,' he said. 'You might have caught something.'

'I fixed him,' said Lancaster. 'I ran after him and called out "Robert." He was so surprised at anyone using his name he dropped all the books he was carrying.'

They were in the middle of the courtyard, scrabbling on the ground for the scattered library books.

'Sorry,' said Robert, 'sorry about this.'

'Not at all,' said Henry. 'I'm the one who should be apologising.'

'No, no, my fault,' insisted Robert.

'No.'

'Absolutely.'

Not at all.'

'I insist.'

It could have gone on for ever, like a romantic tone poem that would not end, like one of Robert's lectures, spluttering into staccato incoherence.

His first lecture had been a nightmare. He was in a state of terror.

'First night nerves, you know,' he said. 'Rushed out of my room. Down to the lecture theatre. Sea of faces. Like ancient Rome. Waiting for the lions to be released. Opened my folder. Nothing there.'

The abysm.

'Mind went blank. Thought I'd died. Relief in a way. Wouldn't have to lecture.'

But the sounds of rustling newspapers and chewing on sandwiches brought him back to reality.

He rushed back to his room. Found the right folder. Set off again.

'And then, wouldn't you know, something held me back. It was like a hand grabbing me, stopping me from getting there.

So I gave a decisive push forward and there was this awful ripping noise. It was my gown, caught in the door. Ripped to shreds, all in tatters. Had to wear it. Too late to change. Then when I got back to the lecture theatre I poured a glass of water to steady my nerves. Think it must have been in the jug for a couple of weeks. Tasted foul. Choked on it and spilled it all down my shirt.

'Caused an uproar, of course. Funny thing, you never think students take any notice of anything. But they noticed this. Hilarious to them. Never lectured in a gown since.'

Then there was the time of power cuts and electricity shortages.

'Damn unions,' said Gervaise. 'They should bring in the troops. That would show them.'

'You should volunteer,' said Pawley. 'It would be like the heady days of the Miners' Strike again. Pouring champagne over the heads of the proletariat. Relive your youthful idealism.'

Robert blundered in, spilled his tea on the common room table, dropped his biscuit on the floor. He brushed the biscuit off on his scarf before eating it.

'Have you been having blackouts?' asked Pawley.

'Me?' he said.

His cup shook in his hand and he scattered more drops.

'No. No, not at all. I've been pretty well for a while.'

'Looks like you're all rugged up for the cold,' said Pawley.

'All drugged up? No, no, not at the moment, doctor's taken me off the pills.'

'I meant your scarf and coat.'

'Oh. Ha ha.' He laughed and spilled the rest of the tea over Gervaise's deck shoes.

He tried to mop it up with his scarf but forgot to unwrap it from his neck first. As he tugged at the end and pulled himself down to reach the shoes, it knotted round his throat and proceeded to choke him. His face reddened.

'*As I Lay Dying?*' suggested Dr Bee. 'Anyone else for charades.'

Gervaise got up and left. Pawley leaned over and loosened Robert's scarf.

'Close shave,' he said.

'New blade,' said Robert. 'Cut myself this morning,' he added, pointing to the various gashes and serrations on his jaw.

Once in a while when it all got too much he went away for treatment. The lectures opened into an ever deepening abyss, the chewing students seemed more ravening than ever, the sheer hostility of the environment undermined him.

'He's a sensitive,' said Pawley. 'He's our canary in the coalmine. He smells the poisonous gasses before the rest of us. We should value him. As the job gets worse we should be warned by him.'

'That's not what you said when you went to share a house with him,' said Dr Bee.

'That was different,' said Pawley. 'I'd only just arrived. I asked about accommodation and someone said Robert had a house he wanted to share.'

'And you leaped at it.'

'I'm not sure I exactly leaped,' said Pawley. 'But I was interested. Problem was he couldn't find it. We set off from campus to have a look and he got lost on the way. I never did see it. We spent an hour wandering around these back streets. And it wasn't like some place he was renting out. He lived there himself. He must have gone there every day.'

'Unless he never found it and slept out rough,' said Dr Bee. 'Or stayed in the department and shared a hammock with Gervaise.'

Robert came back refreshed from a spell in hospital.

'All rather jolly,' he said to Pawley. 'Lots of drugs. Just your cup of tea.'

'Sounds appealing,' agreed Pawley. 'What about electric shocks.'

'No, didn't get that,' said Robert. 'Not that I can remember. Just group therapy.'

'What's that like?'

'Much like a tutorial,' said Robert.

He was the one person they could all feel superior to, the one person they could all feel was less competent than themselves. Their scapegoat. It was only when he announced he was taking early retirement that they realised how necessary he was to them, how essential he was to the health of the department, their only source of self esteem in the great demoralisation.

But the climate of unease had got to him. The barrage of questionnaires, the endless requests for self-assessment, the demands for research reports and publication reports, the battery of student evaluation, finally undid whatever running repairs decades of psychotherapy had achieved. He could see the future all too clearly, endless demands for self-justification, endless destabilisation and deconstruction of the laboriously assembled personality.

He quit. He quit even before the early retirement package had been assembled and bonuses were on offer. The first to crack. And with him he took the department's communal confidence. Now there was no one worse off. Now there was no one anyone could point to as demonstrably more distracted, more distrait, less together. Now there was no barrier between the individual and the slavering forces of destruction. It was not even a question of which of them was to be cast in his role. His role had been abolished. Now they were all endlessly vulnerable, total vulnerability was the state of the future.

12

A Famous Edited Book

The ascent of women in the university had been a triumph of the strategies of positive discrimination. If youhad never published anything of significance or never given any conference papers you could get promotion on the grounds of having been oppressed as a woman. At the same time, as a senior academic (female) you were in demand for faculty committees and university committees. The new equal opportunity university, as it announced itself in every advertisement it placed, required female representation on every committee. Since there were so few women in any department outside of the humanities, any calculating careerist could work out a game plan for the new game. Soon Edwina was on every committee that came up.

'They write it up as if it's something to be proud of,' said Dr Bee, dropping the *University Mirror* into the re-cycling bin. 'They run a news story telling us every time she's put on another committee as if it's something admirable. It's an outrage. It's an indictment. How many committee's can you effectively serve on?'

'Never been asked to serve on any,' said Pawley.

'Never had a bar of them,' said Henry Lancaster. 'Waste of time.'

But the new world order saw things differently.

'This is the business of the university now,' said Pawley. 'Committees.'

'I thought you said the business of the university was filling in forms,' said Dr Bee.

'Mixed business,' said Pawley. 'The political principle of the corner shop. The revenge of the petit-bourgeoisie.'

Housekeeping. That was the term recurrently used. The Head of Department would call a meeting, 'to address some housekeeping issues.'

'Should I bring my supermarket trolley?' Dr Bee asked her at morning tea.

Committees were all very well, but somewhere along the line something had to be published. The pressure on research scores had focussed attention on research and publication. The good old days of the gentlemen scholars with nothing in print were hard to sustain. A book, a book. The Head of Department had followed Edwina as a role model into the world of committees, but she nonetheless perceived that she might need a book for the lists after all. Something solid. Something institutional. Something she could cite as a scholarly publication and be given a D. Litt. for and get elected to a couple of Academies on the strength of, and so get Edwina's job when she retired. Any day now.

Not that books were universally accepted, of course. Scientists didn't write books. They produced short articles with multiple authors: every author claimed the research outputs score, and the work itself was done by graduate students and research assistants. The philosophers rarely wrote books either. They preferred enigmatic articles in professional journals. They lobbied for a research score based on five points for an article and seven for a book. 'A book contains eight or ten articles,' Lancaster fulminated. 'How dare they do this?'

For a while the Head of Department thought about hiring someone to write it, or buying something ready-made off the shelf. If that had been good enough for J. F. Kennedy and J. Edgar Hoover it was good enough for her. Download it from the web. But the truth always leaked out in the end. It was too risky. And then it came in a flash as she was reading through a batch of CVs on the promotion committee. What did other people do? People, that was, who didn't get round to writing books either. And there it was. They edited books. She gloated with the glow of an old fossicker on the Ballarat goldfields as the nuggets displayed themselves. Edited books. You edit, others do the writing. Why hadn't she thought of it before? But she thrust down any unwelcome self-criticism. She had thought of it now. The past was history and to be discarded. The future is ours, sisters.

Of course the first flush of discovery faded as it always does. It faded as the gloom of substance spread across the horizon. Substance, subject, what was it to be about? What could she edit a book on? It might all have died there and her hopes with it.

Salvation came as she was standing in the courtyard one evening, the twilight fading after the last of the day's committees. Bats stumbled in a daze amidst the eclectic jumble of old Brutalist and neo-educational-Ruskinian facades. The Dead Hand hobbled in and out of the replica Parisian pissoir he favoured.

'Look at him,' said Edwina in disgust, 'flies wide open, piss all over his shoes.'

She strode off, leaving the Head of Department standing there. The Dead Hand lumbered up.

'She's looking her age,' he said with rare cheerfulness, watching the departing Edwina.

It was not a topic the Head of Department would initiate, but she was happy to let it run. 'She's not been well,' she said, in a tone that might have been sympathetic or might have been smarmy.

'How long's she got?'

'One year, three months, eleven days.'

'I wonder who will replace her,' said the Dead Hand, surely not innocently.

The Head of Department stood silent. I am she, I am she, she proclaimed silently. Out of the graveyard of literature and into serious administration.

'I suppose we ought to make some sort of gesture,' said the Dead Hand. 'To mark her going. After all, she used to be one of us.'

It was unclear to the Head of Department whether he meant a male, or a literature professor. But she agreed with the suggestion. Anything to help Edwina on her way, ease her out.

A tribute.

'We could have a farewell dinner,' said the Head of Department. 'Everybody bring a plate.'

Good housekeeping.

'Don't you think it ought to be something more than sandwiches?' said the Dead Hand. 'Something more enduring. Something of substance.'

Substance. It triggered an association in the back of the Head of Department's memory. Something uneasy. Something distressing. Substance. A subject. It came out before she could stop it. That irrepressible anxiety.

'A book.'

'A book?' said the Dead Hand, with unfeigned puzzlement.

'I know, they're boring, horrible things. But it doesn't have to be a long one.'

'You think we should buy one for her? To read in her retirement? Large print?'

'No, I wasn't thinking of that.'

'You don't mean write a book? About her?'

'No, not write one,' she said. 'Heaven forbid.

'What then?'

'I was thinking more of editing something.'

And then the Dead Hand saw. 'An edited book?' he said. 'You mean essays in her honour, that sort of thing?'

The Head of Department hadn't. But she did now. 'That's it.' She fumbled for the term. Anything to avoid saying the book word again. 'A festschrift.'

'For when she goes,' said the Dead Hand.

And I get her job, thought the Head of Department.

She gazed at him in pure joy.

'Not a bad idea,' said the Dead Hand.

'Your idea,' said the Head of Department.

'No, yours,' said the Dead Hand.

'Well, ours then,' said the Head of Department, all faculties functioning. 'Ours. We could do it together.' There it was. The D. Litt. And get the Dead Hand to do all the work on the beastly thing.

But the Dead Hand had already seen that catch.

'It's not really my cup of tea,' he said. 'No, you do it. You need it more than I do. I've already edited one.' No point in doing another, once he had a chair.

The Head of Department looked alarmed. It wasn't her cup of tea either. If he had suggested a video she might have bought it. But a book? This was the new millennium. Beyond the book. As soon as she had edited one, she would get well beyond it.

'Get Philippa on board,' the Dead of Hand said. 'She knows about that sort of thing.'

The Head of Department still looked dubious.

'She knows how to get a publisher. And how to proof-read.

She'll be good for the leg-work.'

The Head of Department had heard about publishers and proof-reading on the Library Committee. And the Intellectual Property Committee. And the Committee to Close Down the University Press. If that was what was needed, she would co-opt Philippa.

'She'll be perfect.'

The sunset glowed erogenously around them. The Italianate tower burst into wheezing, juddering spasm as the clock struck the hour. And so the idea was conceived.

Selecting the contributors was a delight. The pleasures of exclusion. Who not to invite. And the pleasures of inclusion too, the charm of extending patronage, do you want to be in my team? It was like back in the school gym again, all sweat and towels and communal showers. Picking your team. I'll have her and her and her. Leaving the runts out there in a rejected, huddled mass.

So they drew up a list. Or rather Philippa drew it up while the Head of Department called out names from behind her desk. No point being a Head of Department unless you could dictate to somebody across a desk. And Head of Department desks were something special, fifty per cent more desk than the standard academic staff issue.

Distinguished former students, distinguished former colleagues, less distinguished former students and former colleagues, current colleagues. It cause a flurry round the department.

'Write something !' said Dr Bee. 'Who's going to be able to do that?'

'Well –,' Lancaster began.

'Not I,' said Dr Bee. 'There's far too much in print already.'

'Well –,' said Lancaster.

'Oh, I'm sure you will, Henry,' said Dr Bee. 'Scribble, scribble, scribble, heh? But what about our less logorrheic colleagues?

Those without the benefit of frontal lobe epilepsy?'

'Well –,' Lancaster tried again.

Dr Bee ignored him.

'It will be back to the student body yet once more,' he said. 'All those fluent students they're always accusing of plagiarism will now find themselves plagiarised. The photocopier will be running hot as student essays are surreptitiously stolen. Or the scanner. They'll put them through the scanner so they're available straight onto disk. I forget our high-tech world.'

But for Lancaster it was not a matter of jest. It tormented him. How could he contribute to a volume of tributes for Deadwood Edwina? The depths of his horror were inexpressible even through the embodiments of the appalling in his own fiction. He would have had to have written Gothic to have approached the extent of his feelings. Perhaps I should, he thought. There's a market there.

'She's beyond words. She's like a vampire that has no image in a mirror. She's the ultimate black hole. You try to write about her and the screen goes blank. Nothing comes out. She's the embodiment of absence. Total negation.'

'You've tried?' said Dr Bee.

'Of course I've tried. I know, I know, why give immortality to someone like that?'

'You have the gift of conferring immortality?' asked Dr Bee.

'But I thought if I could just write her out of my system I might forget about her. Once you've written about something it ceases to worry you. It's like therapy. But with Edwina, she's inécritable.'

'Inécritable?'

'It's a neologism,' said Lancaster.

'Clearly,' said Dr Bee.

'But a festschrift. Essays in her honour. What honour? How can I write something for the embodiment of all I oppose? How could I live with myself?'

'You'll find a way,' said Dr Bee.

'How can you not?' said Pawley. 'If you refuse they'll never forget. It will be seen as a calculated insult.'

'That's the idea,' said Lancaster.

'Are you sure that's what you want? It will be recorded against you for eternity. An insult to the University, to the Pro-Vice-Chancellor and to the Head of Department. All three. Bang goes any hope of a personal chair. No honorary D. Litt. No more study leave. You'll probably end up with ten first year tutorials.'

'Oh, the evil of it,' said Lancaster.

'Anyway,' said Pawley, 'how can you turn down a free publication? I look on festschriften like a charity concert. They can't knock you back if they invite you. They ask you to write so you write. You write something you could never get published otherwise. They can't refuse it.'

But they could. And did. The pleasures of rejection, oh the pleasures of rejection. Pawley's piece on the history of hashish in literature was deemed inappropriate. Too historical. This was a literary volume.

'Homer,' he said, 'Rabelais, Dumas, Baudelaire, Gautier, Balzac, Flaubert, the Thousand and One Nights.'

'Ah, but English literature,' Philippa explained. 'They're all, well, foreigners.'

It took him a thousand and one joints to calm down. He sat in his room seething, eyes glaring like Beowulf's mother, enveloped in smoke like a djinn in a bottle.

Lancaster rescued him.

'Are you replicating the death of Zola in here?' he said, choking in the fug, flinging open the windows. 'You have to have oxygen. It's a basic principle of life.'

'I blocked the bottom of the door so the smoke wouldn't

spread down the corridor,' said Pawley, indicating the sand-filled draft-stopper. 'Not that I care. Why should I care? The indignity of it. What do I have to lose?'

'All those pension contributions,' said Lancaster.

Pawley went into a paroxysm of coughing.

'Well yes,' conceded Lancaster, 'you probably won't live to benefit. What have you to lose after all?'

'So what did you contribute? Rip out a chapter of a novel lying by?'

'I thought of it. No. Too good to waste on her. I agonised for weeks. Months. I'd wake up in the middle of the night thinking, I can't contribute to this. Then I'd wake up realising, I can't not. They'd take it as a gesture.'

'They know what you think, anyway.'

'I suppose they do. But not in writing.'

'If you didn't contribute it wouldn't be in writing. It would be in absence.'

'No difference in these post-structuralist days,' said Lancaster. 'Absence is as good as presence. Look at what their careers are based on. Utter invisibility'

'So you gave them something.'

'What could I do? I'd thought of a cancelled chapter. Something I'd thrown out. But I wouldn't want something like that in print. It would be a nice gesture but it would reflect back on me, wouldn't it? It was a nightmare. I've never sweated so much on anything. I could've written a novel in the time I wasted agonising about it. A trilogy. Without a doubt. Easily. I shall never forgive them for the torture they put me through. That was probably the intention. Subconsciously. I'm sure subconsciously the whole thing was designed to torture people. No one wanted to write in honour of her but no one dared not.'

'So what did you give them?'

'I used a piece I'd published in Belgrade. I mean I'd written it for a conference there and they translated it for the conference proceedings. The English version never appeared. Got bombed by NATO. Seemed a shame to waste it. Couldn't face the thought of doing something new for that creature. No one will ever know. And if they do, who cares? It will show what I think of the whole business.'

'I thought that's what you didn't want to show.'

'I don't know any more,' said Lancaster. 'I really don't know.'

The School of Business Studies Board-room was booked for the presentation ceremony, the best that money could buy. This would be the moment of glory. For the Head of Department and Philippa. For Edwina, too, of course. But for the Head of Department and Philippa especially. A book, a book. All the sisterhood and their committee cronies were on the guest list and would see it. Edwina's farewell gift, a touching memento to mark her retirement.

Except that she was not about to retire.

The Head of Department, who like most of her colleagues had taken up literature because she had no skills in maths or languages, had miscalculated Edwina's age by a couple of years.

'I'm not that old, darling,' Edwina said, when the Head of Department foreshadowed the planned occasion. 'By all means go ahead with the presentation of the book. That would be simply lovely. But don't advertise it as a farewell. I'm not thinking of retiring yet. Not now there's no longer any compulsory retirement age for senior management. I expect to be here for years.'

The Head of Department's cup and saucer shook as she put them rapidly down on the table. She couldn't trust herself to speak.

'How can we have a retirement presentation if she won't retire?' asked the Head of Department.

'It makes it difficult,' agreed Philippa

'I'll cancel it,' said the Head of Department.

'And the book?' asked Philippa.

'I'll cancel it too.'

'Are you sure?'

'There aren't any funds to subsidise it, anyway. And you said yourself, none of the publishers you approached will touch it unless we offer them hard cash. We'd have to take the money out of the visiting lecturers account and I've already committed that for part-time tutors for teaching relief.'

Since the Head of Department had served with Edwina on the stream of committees for closing down the university press, the book publications subsidies and the journals assistance scheme, she could talk confidently of the absence of available funding. They had both argued against supporting those who produced. It was discriminatory. Destroyed forests, too.

'I'm not sure I'm strongly motivated to put in any more effort.'

Philippa, who had been doing the editing, wondered how much effort the Head of Department thought she had put in.

'Still, it seems a pity to waste all that work,' said Philippa. Her work.

The Head of Department shrugged. She wasn't sure she'd ever been that keen on the idea of a book, anyway. Smart of the Dead Hand to sidestep it. He knew a thing or two, clearly. And not from books.

'There are funds for technological innovation,' Philippa said. 'We can do it electronically. Put it on the web.'

'Really?' said the Head of Department.

'Easy.'

'And it still counts as a publication?'

'Of course.'

'How brilliant.'

'It is, isn't it? It saves paying out good money to print a pile of books we'd never sell anyway. They'd just rot in some forgotten storeroom. And we don't need to hire a room to present it to Edwina. We can just e-mail it to her.'

They embraced, ecstatically.

'I imagine she looked up Edwina's date of birth in a *Who's Who*,' said Pawley.

'And they're guaranteed to be wrong, are they?' said Lancaster, an avid filler in of forms for any biographical or bibliographical reference book.

'Usually,' said Pawley. 'The subjects provide their own data, and most people fake them.'

'And why would they do that?'

'To prevent anyone from working out their astrological chart and doing black magic on them.'

Lancaster blenched. 'You can't be serious.'

Pawley was no less shocked at Lancaster's reaction. 'You haven't been giving them your real date of birth, Henry? In all those writers' directories? No wonder your career is plummeting.'

Lancaster drew himself up, as far as he could beneath the pressing weight of sudden despair. 'It is not plummeting.'

'It's not exactly soaring.'

'She probably lopped off a couple of years along with the rest of it in the sex-change operation,' said Dr Bee. 'Personally if I were going to fake it I'd add on a couple to get earlier retirement.'

'The whole point is she doesn't want to retire,' said Pawley. 'She wants to stay for ever.'

'Spare us,' said Lancaster.

'I don't think she will,' said Dr Bee.

'So we have a retirement tribute for someone who is not going to retire and a book that is not a book,' said Lancaster.

'A virtual festschrift,' said Pawley.

‘A virtual tribute,’ agreed Dr Bee. ‘In virtual honour.’

‘Who says there is no justice?’ said Pawley. ‘Think how our poor Head of Department must be feeling. She’s suffered the cruellest blow. The ingratitude of it. Equity and affirmative action would undeniably have shunted her into Edwina’s shoes, but Edwina refuses to take them off. She’s positioned herself to take on the mantle and Edwina refuses to disrobe. What’s the betting she’ll scratch out her eyes at the rape-bus bus-stop? Or bash her to a pulp in the gym? Or lure her to the genetic engineering department and lock her up with the viruses over the weekend?’

‘To what avail?’ asked Dr Bee. ‘You know it’s virtually impossible to kill the virtual dead.’

13

Hey Ho

Suddenly Rowley was back. The harassment tribunal had collapsed in disarray and there he was once more.

'Who is this Rowley, whose word no man relies on?' asked Dr Bee.

'Our third man. Or is it fifth man? The missing diplomat. The man in exile on the shores of Lake Como. The corresponding member of the Academy of Lagado.'

Rowley was the third chair but everybody had repressed his existence.

'I haven't,' said Lancaster. 'I remember his existence vividly. I was in for that job if you remember.'

'As I remember you've been in for many a job,' said Dr Bee. 'Why single out this one?'

'Because it was an outrage,' said Lancaster.

'Aren't they all an outrage?'

'Yes,' said Lancaster. 'But this was a particularly outrageous outrage. They had the hide to ask me, "If you were appointed to the chair, how long would you stay?"'

'And you answered?'

'I said I'd been in this damn hole twenty-three years and I could see no reason why I'd move on if I got the chair.'

'Ah,' said Pawley.

'Oh dear,' said Dr Bee.

'That was your mistake,' said Pawley.

'You should have told them that you would leave immediately.'

'Within two years at most.'

'That you were just using it as a stepping stone to something greater.'

'They'd have given it you like a shot if they'd thought they were getting rid of you,' said Pawley.

'And you know what they did?' said Lancaster.

'Yes,' they said. All too well.

He disregarded them. 'You know what they did? They appointed this damned bounder who's always somewhere else.'

'Of course,' said Pawley.

'And now he's never here.'

'Exactly what they wanted,' said Dr Bee.

Rowley's first grand scheme was to team up with Gervaise to catch the new wave of Collaborative Research Projects and they landed a Large Grant. Perhaps it was a trusting belief in Gervaise's boating skill that lay behind the alliance. Perhaps they had served in the same SAS unit for their national service. Whatever it was, they cooked up a proposal to trace the early wanderings of Joseph Conrad round the Gulf of Thailand and the South China Sea. The methodology seemed to consist of looking for dusky young native girls with wild Slavic eyes.

The rumors came back before they did. It was whispered they were smuggling out stolen art works from Angkor Wat and such like temples. Rowley's next door neighbour ran a gallery and had international connections. Their ship was boarded and the story hit the press, briefly, before it mysteriously died. Gervaise and Rowley both went on leave to cooler spots for a year.

It was a splendid scandal but Pawley wanted a better one.

'All cover,' he said confidently. 'They were checking out Islamic guerillas. Drawing up a list of opponents to minerals and oil exploitation. Monitoring Chinese and Indonesian naval communications. A classic Department of Foreign Affairs project on behalf of the international military-industrial complex. Why else would the vice-chancellor pick up the tab for the legal expenses?'

While he was away Rowley acquired another Large Grant and hired a couple of research assistants, Tom S. Eliot and E. Pound. It worked well for a year until some clerk in the accounts office noticed Tom S. Eliot's address and E. Pound's address were the same as Rowley's own. Rowley proved unable to produce the assistants in the flesh, burst into tears and pleaded mental breakdown after the stress of the art works incident. The university chose not to prosecute and Rowley went off to Virginia on sick leave.

His next project was to lever himself back to the Old World on the strength of his chair. Hours on the phone and endless e-mails were eventually rewarded. He landed six months a year teaching at some Italian university and off he went. Inexorably the six months extended to seven, eight. He came back for his semester, trimming off the first week, and leaving in the week before the end.

'How does he get away with it?' asked Lancaster.

'You want to stop him?' said Dr Bee. 'You would prefer him to be here?'

'It's the principle of the thing,' said Lancaster.

'There are no principles,' said Dr Bee. 'And any principle that meant we had Rowley here any more than we do would be a bad one.'

Now Rowley was back and enraged. He bobbed in and out of his room, the door wedged open with an unexamined PhD thesis, intercepting anyone who went down the corridor.

'They've halved my salary,' he boomed. 'They've cut me back. It's a disgrace. They've put me on half pay.'

'But you're only here half time. If that,' said Dr Bee.

'That's not the point,' said Rowley. 'It's just like their damn cheek.'

He bounced up and down in fury, his Italian ice-cream seller's seersucker suit strobing like a lightshow from the sixties.

'When I find out who did this,' Rowley threatened.

'Let us know how you manage,' said Dr Bee. 'I've never been able to find out who did anything in this place.'

'I'll bet it was that damned whore,' said Rowley.

'Which particular one?'

'The Head of Department. Doing her busybodying housekeeping. Wait till she applies for another Large Grant. I'll make sure I'm her assessor. I'll give her nought out of a hundred. That'll fix her.'

'If only I could believe it would,' said Dr Bee.

'Do you mean to tell me,' said Lancaster, 'that Rowley's been on full professorial salary and only teaching half the year?'

'Four months of the year, I think you'll find,' said Dr Bee.

'How do these things happen?' asked Lancaster.

'Nice work if you can get it,' said Pawley.

'But how do you get it?'

'Ah,' said Pawley, 'Nudge, nudge, wink, wink.'

'What, sexual favours?' said Lancaster.

'Could be,' said Pawley. 'Though I was thinking more of secret service work. But that tends to overlap with sexual favours. Someone must have been protecting him. They needed a sleeper on the shores of Lake Como.'

'Oh, you and your conspiracies,' said Lancaster.

'Not my conspiracies,' said Pawley.

But Lancaster was too enraged to engage. The thought of Rowley spending eight months of the year on Lake Como, drawing a second salary for teaching English as a foreign language, was too much to bear.

'Think what I could do with an arrangement like that,' he said. 'Think of the novels I could write if I had eight months of the year away on full salary.'

'But are we ready for them?' asked Dr Bee.

14

Early Retirement

The Head of Department stood outside the steps of the department building handing out early retirement notices.

'Like she was Colonel Pride purging parliament,' said Dr Bee.

'Or a boa constrictor warming up in the sun,' said Pawley, momentarily flexing a genially green consciousness after a handful of early morning joints.

'Something herpetic we are agreed,' said Henry Lancaster, 'genitally herpetic.'

'Did she give one out to everyone?' asked Dr Bee.

'I think she targeted us,' said Pawley.

'Doesn't she realise she too will reach the targeted age?' said Dr Bee. 'Does she believe time will stop for her?'

'Assassins never imagine someone will assassinate them,' said Pawley. 'Otherwise they'd never do the job. But someone always gets them. Every time.' Still genial at the thought of it.

'I can't wait to see it,' said Lancaster. 'I find it offensive to be greeted by a scarcely veiled threat first thing in the morning.'

'She seems to be fully dressed to me,' said Dr Bee. 'And I don't think she'd think eleven o'clock was first thing. She's probably been standing there since seven. You can tell how early she gets in by the way she gets her four-wheel drive in the parking spot nearest the door. You have to be in before the attendants to get that one.'

'What I don't understand - ' said Lancaster.

'This could take some time,' said Dr Bee.

'Is how on the one hand they are trying to push people out into early retirement, and at the same time they abolish the compulsory retirement age. It's utterly contradictory. It makes no sense at all.'

'Oh yes it does,' said Pawley. 'The contradictions make it quite clear what they're up to. They're targeting people like us. Our age. Contaminated by the sixties and seventies.'

'Speak for yourself,' said Dr Bee. 'I deny contamination by anything.'

'But you were around then,' said Pawley.

'He certainly was,' said Lancaster. 'The Casanova of the student canteen. Around anything that moved, and much that didn't.'

'Anyone who was around in the sixties and seventies is contaminated as far as they are concerned,' said Pawley.

'And this they?' asked Dr Bee.

'The Ministry. The administration.'

'Senior Management you have to call it now,' said Lancaster.

'People of our generation know there are different ways to do things. We saw authority challenged.'

'Red bases on campus,' said Dr Bee.

'The Free University,' said Lancaster.

'Open decision making,' said Dr Bee.

'Students on departmental committees,' said Lancaster.

'You may mock,' said Pawley.

'We certainly do,' said Dr Bee.

'You may mock, but all those things threatened the old authoritarian structures. Now they want the structures back in place. They're terrified that anyone who was around in the sixties and seventies still has an agenda of reform. So they want to clear us all out with early retirement incentives. If we don't go they've got a problem. We're now the age we would normally be running the show. So to stop that happening they've abolished the retirement age so the boring old bastards who've kept things dead and inert for decades can stay in place till the generation below us is ready to take over from them. That way they cut us out altogether.'

'Plausible,' said Lancaster.

'What other explanation is there?' asked Pawley. 'Why else let Edwina stay on? They need her and the rest of the dead wood holding the fort till they've fixed up the next bunch of toadies with chairs and enough committee experience to put them in place.'

'Like our Head of Department.'

'Like Philippa.'

The campaign was well orchestrated. Before the early retirement offer went out there had been a steady build up of pressure. The endless reports to be filled in with details of publications, of research, of research grants received, of community activities, created a climate of unease. It was simple enough to disregard one request for information. But when the requests came in week after week the determination of even the strong began to be worn down. Anxiety crept in, the sense of having nothing to report cut through even the thickest skins. Gervaise could be seen growling and gesturing and filing the latest request in one of the paper-recycling bags scattered around the building, and then fifteen minutes later rummaging through the rubbish to retrieve it. Others were starting to worry. Pawley played on their fears, part of his ongoing project to bring society to its knees by a process of demystification and imaginative paranoia.

'Community activities,' he said. 'They're very dodgy. If you don't fill any in then the Community Relations office will summon you in for counselling. But if you fill in too many at some point somebody's going to ask, How come this person has the time for all these community activities? Are they doing any academic work? Never mind the Boy Scouts and the Volunteer Fire Brigade, let's look at their research record. Is there any? Let's look at their activities report. How much teaching do they do?'

He would hound them down the corridors, remorselessly analysing every aspect of it.

'And what sort of community activities? How about your membership of the Friends of Greater Serbia, Henry? Do you really want to list that? That will be sent straight on to the security services, I'd think, wouldn't you?'

The health questionnaire was another dubious one. At least in Pawley's eyes. And in Dr Bee's too. How much physical activity do you do? Would you consider yourself fit, very fit, unfit? Do you run, jog, swim, cycle, play squash, tennis, football . . . .?

'None of their damn business,' wheezed Dr Bee, choking with stress induced rage, purple in the face, cardiac arrest imminent.

Even the questionnaire on questionnaires, foreshadowed by Pawley's herbally accelerated wit, caused no joy when it materialised in all humorless actuality.

'Do you find the questions of the review relevant, irrelevant, or don't know? Do you find the issues addressed adequate? Do you - '

'It has to be a fraud,' said Henry. 'It has to be a talentless parody. How can they do it?'

But they could, and did. Every week another request for information would come through, another needling disturbance into a fragile equanimity, another reminder that some other aspect of the job was being looked at. This is not the job it was when you were first employed. Are you sure you really want to stay in it? How much stress and destabilisation can you take? Wouldn't the early retirement package be a better option? Why not phone up Human Resources Management now and make an appointment?

And then there was the staff development review. This was a sell-out engineered by the Union for a two percent pay increase. Everyone now had to be reviewed annually. And once again go through their teaching activities, publications, research, research grants and health in confidence with the Head of Department, or some other person designated as an approved staff development review officer. To become such a person you had to attend a two-day training course at the old quarantine station.

'It would be a fine irony,' said Dr Bee, 'if development review turned out to be just another synonym for termination procedures. "You have failed your development review so you are now terminated."'

'With extreme prejudice,' said Pawley.

'Of course,' said Dr Bee. 'What other way is there?'

And again, like all the other endless reports and reviews and questionnaires, it had its major role as an anxiety inducing agent, inciting staff to self-destruct before even facing the review, driving them into submitting their resignations rather than face an hour in one to one session with the Dead Hand or the Head of Department or their ilk in other departments.

Gervaise came back from study leave in a profane rage. What he'd been studying no one ever knew. But he'd been in Peru or Perugia or somewhere, somewhere where he had given the fax number of the local coffee shop – 'lovely little place I've discovered, off the beaten track a bit' - somewhere where they charged you for faxes received, for the amount of paper consumed. The Head of Department had faxed him the early retirement document in full and it had cost him a fortune to receive it.

'Harassment, that's what it is,' he said.

But there was worse to come. She sent round a memo that everyone over fifty-five was to attend counselling on early retirement opportunities.

Gervaise spent a week drafting a complaint to the discrimination committee about ageist harassment. The compulsory counselling scheme was silently dropped.

But it had set him thinking. He could feel the pressures all too palpably.

'It's a conspiracy,' he announced. 'They plan to get rid of all us males. We are in the way of the femocrats and they take no prisoners. This isn't gender balance, this is genocide. Gender cleansing.'

The official story was that they were overstaffed. The Ministry had established new guidelines, parameters, playing fields.

'Does that mean we've been losing students?' asked Gervaise.

'No, no, no, not at all,' said the Head of Department.

'Gaining students?'

'It's nothing to do with that.'

'So what are these magic figures?'

'There's nothing magic as you call it,' she snapped. 'The Ministry has established an overall ratio of staff to students.'

'On the basis of what?'

'It would take too long to explain now. If you ever went to faculty meetings you would know.'

'I doubt it,' said Gervaise.

'The Department has been asked to calculate how many

positions it needs to cut.'

'I'd think none,' said Gervaise. 'We should ask for more.'

'We can't ask for more,' said the Head of Department.

'Never cut your own throat when there are other people ready to do it,' said Gervaise.

'Just bare the neck and lie on your back, is that your advice?' said Pawley.

'We have to come up with proposals,' said the Head of Department.

'I fail to see why,' said Gervaise.

'Because if we don't faculty will do it for us.'

'Let them,' said Gervaise.

'Then we shall be much worse off.'

'I find that hard to imagine,' said Gervaise.

But in the end the meeting agreed. It always agreed. There was never a vote. Consensus. Consensus was whatever the Dead Hand had cooked up with the Head of Department beforehand.

'So we voluntarily offer to shed five to seven positions,' said Gervaise.

'I thought it was twelve,' said Pawley.

'Twelve was what she said we should shed. Five to seven was what we are proposing.'

'Is it five or is it seven?' asked Dr Bee.

'Depends on how you behave,' said Pawley. 'Depends whether she's got you marked down in the first five or whether you're in the probationary two.'

Over the weeks and months, of course, the numbers changed. It was like Senator McCarthy's allegations of the number of communists in the state department, a calculated inconsistency that added to the climate of fear. It wasn't possible to relax in the knowledge that there was a set number and the purge would stop there. The purge was elastic, protean. It could always be extended to take in someone else. No one was safe, except those instigating and operating it. And even they might end up vulnerable, if history was to be believed. Not that they believed in history. History and pre-modern literature were on the agenda for purging too.

'It's nonsense to say it's economic forces,' said Pawley. 'Look how much money's being splashed around. Look how much they spent on buying another house for the Vice-Chancellor. Look at the financial packages they give him and Senior Management.'

'We can't look at them,' said Dr Bee. 'The figures are never made public.'

'Shouldn't they be made public if they're paid for from public funds?' said Henry. 'Tax-payers' money and all that?'

'Twenty years ago,' said Pawley, 'there was one person in administration for six teaching staff. Now it's one administrator for every one teaching position. That doesn't count all those academic staff who spend their entire time on administrative committees and get teaching relief so they never do any teaching.'

'Soon,' said Dr Bee, 'it will be like the American military. Twelve support staff for every man in the field.'

'And they don't even issue us with drugs,' said Pawley. 'At least the American troops in Vietnam were stoned all the time.'

'You seem to manage,' said Dr Bee.

'And they used to kill their own officers,' said Pawley. 'Lob a grenade into the tent of some bastard they hated.'

They mused on the possibility in the afternoon light, the clatter of helicopters overhead, the gentle scent of cannabis exuding from Pawley's saturated hair and clothing, the poisonous chemicals wafting through the windows from the departments of chemistry and pharmacy and biology and psychology, the stretch limousines ferrying in men in button-down shirts across campus to the American Center.

Finance was the excuse. Budgetary considerations. But anyone who wanted to could see that that was only an excuse. Most didn't want to. They were already so fearful, demoralised or sycophantic they wanted to see nothing. The climate of insecurity was having its effect. Destabilising the academics, unnerving the already pretty well nerveless, it made central control easier to reimpose. Tenure could not be removed without a public battle. But an inexorable process of destabilisation could make the job so anxiety ridden and unpleasant that staff would voluntarily surrender and rush out into retirement.

'You can't rush out of a cemetery,' said Dr Bee. 'At least not until judgement day.'

'This is judgement day,' said Pawley. 'This is the apocalypse. These are the last days. The days of rapture. What they plan now is to have all the new staff on short term contracts. Then if they say anything out of line, chop, out you go.'

'If they say anything, I'd imagine,' said Dr Bee.

'Once you've got your staff on contract, you have total control. No one will dare complain. No one will step out of line. It's the end of any idea of academic freedom.'

'What was this idea of academic freedom?' asked Dr Bee. 'I never saw any signs of it.'

'It was an ideal,' said Pawley.

'An ideal nobody ever dared test,' said Dr Bee.

'True,' agreed Pawley. 'In theory it meant you couldn't be sacked or suspended or otherwise discriminated against for your beliefs.'

'Just given ten first year tutorials.'

'That's one way,' said Pawley. 'The other is to try and demoralise you by taking all your teaching away.'

'I should be so lucky,' said Dr Bee.

'I was down to an hour a week one year,' said Pawley, 'after the Dead Hand decided he didn't like what he'd heard I'd been saying. But the money still rolled in. If I'd been on contract I wouldn't have been renewed.'

'In Britain,' said Henry.

'Ah, you're back from the airport,' said Dr Bee. 'Tell us about your latest triumphal trip.'

'In Britain if you get promoted you automatically go onto contract. So some people aren't even applying for promotion. They figure it's safer to stay on tenure.'

'Never thought I had much hope of promotion anyway,' said Dr Bee.

'Nor I,' said Pawley.

'The people I worry about are the young ones,' said Lancaster. 'The one's who will never know tenure.'

'Henry,' said Dr Bee, 'these visits to the old world produce some disgusting humbug from you. You don't have to try and persuade us. None of us cares about the young ones. As long as tenure survives for us, that's all we care about. No one is going to fight for the future generations.'

And that was the deal and everyone knew it. As long as current staff were not threatened with loss of tenure, they wouldn't make any complaints about its removal for new staff. Management proposed it, the union agreed, and everyone kept quiet.

'Solidarity,' said Pawley.

For as long as anyone could remember Henry had been holding forth about his other life, the literary life, and as soon as he could he would retire and become that much vaunted figure, a 'full time writer.'

'But you are a full time writer anyway,' said Dr Bee. 'It's just that you claim a full time salary from this place as well.'

'But to be free,' said Henry.

'On a pension.'

'Of course,' said Henry. 'What is freedom without the financial wherewithal?'

He had made endless phone calls to the superannuation board asking for the latest calculations on what he was worth, what was the optimum age to go. But now the pressure was on to go, now that every momentary whim of departure was being facilitated, he drew back. A combination of natural perversity, low cunning and the novelist's accumulated years of suspicion from dealing with publishers made him reconsider.

'I don't think I'll take this early retirement scheme after all,' he announced. 'I like it here.'

The Dead Hand and the Head of Department looked at him in alarm.

'Kingsley Amis,' said Dr Bee. 'His third novel. Published in 1958.'

The Dead Hand and the Head of Department rushed off to the bank.

'It's the only solution,' said Henry said.

'The final one?' asked Dr Bee.

'Absolutely. If you say you like it here, what can they do? They can't make you retire.'

'They can make your life a misery,' said Gervaise, pocketing a couple of biscuits on his way out of the common room.

'I thought you said your ex-wife had already done that,' said Dr Bee.

'That's right,' said Gervaise. His face lightened. 'So she did. Nothing could be worse than that.'

'No need to be excessive,' said Dr Bee.

'No, he's right,' said Henry. 'The answer is think positive. Say how happy we are. We'll never leave. Like Edwina and the Dead Hand. What can they do?'

'You tell us,' said Dr Bee.

'All they can do is make you a better offer. They have to pay more to get us out. No point taking the piddling little package they offer. No, we have to show how much we love it here. What a heart wrench it would be to leave. What an emotional upset. Nothing less than a quarter of a million.'

'Make up for what your wife and the lawyers took, hey Gervaise?' said Dr Bee.

'Need more than that,' said Gervaise. 'And she'd probably claim on anything I got now. No point my asking for more money. No point my working anyway, she still gets half.'

'No point going on really,' agreed Dr Bee. He took out a box of lozenges. 'Have one of these cyanide pills,' he offered.

Gervaise began making his own contingency plans.

'What we need,' he suggested plangently at the next staff meeting, 'is some provision for staff who volunteer for early retirement. Some honorific title. Honorary research fellow. Honorary associate. Something like that. And a little room. Just somewhere where one can leave one's umbrella and a briefcase.'

'Would there be anything in the briefcase?' the Head of Department asked.

'I'm sure you could always have an inspection at the door of the building,' said Gervaise.

Twenty years earlier Gervaise's briefcase had been stolen with three months' research in it. He traded on the sympathy for a while until people began to ask how much research was three months of Gervaise's research anyway? Indeed, what was his research? He had been working on Conrad's or Lawrence's or Stevenson's or Jack London's Pacific travels for thirty-five years and no one had seen a sign of anything. He had sat on manuscripts, acquired exclusive access to letters and archives, and signed watertight contracts with publishers that had prevented them from assigning his project to anyone else, and prevented anyone else from consulting much of the material. An American scholar had once managed to inveigle himself into Gervaise's study where he had been allowed to look at some of the material on the promise of not making notes. But on leaving he had cracked his head on the doorframe and knocked himself out. When he recovered he remembered nothing. There were those who suspected Gervaise had felled him with an oar or his college cricket bat.

Gervaise took the package. It was known simply as 'the package,' 'early retirement' left unsaid, it was so familiar a concept. Pass the parcel. The letterbomb.

He needed the bonus, he said. And since he had only two more years to go, why not take it? He needed the bonus to buy a little shack to live in now his wife and the lawyers had cleaned him out of everything he owned. Except his boat. He still lived on the boat. There was never any sign of the shack. In rough weather he slung his hammock in his room in the department. This was why he became an honorary research fellow, Dr Bee concluded. So he could continue to have a room in which to sling his hammock. There was certainly no evidence he was doing any research. Though Lancaster reckoned that for a while Gervaise had taken to slinging the hammock in the common-room. Maybe while he was waiting to get the mountings secured into his wall.

'I found it there,' said Lancaster. 'I was cleaning up the place for a reception I gave for the Pan-Pacific writers. Place was a pig-sty. Tucked in one corner was this squalid looking sleeping bag and what I thought was a fishing net. I tossed it all out. I didn't realise what it was at the time. But he must have found it again. It was up in his room the other night. I came in late to pick up a couple of books and his door was open and it was slung across the room. Poor chap.'

'Poor be damned,' said Dr Bee. 'Don't be fooled by Gervaise's pleas of homelessness. He owns a huge house in England which he's kept on so he continues to be a rate-payer and gets his brats free university education there. Before that he'd sent his children back to live with their grandparents for five years so they could claim UK residency and get the local authority to pay their fees and scholarships. He inherited the house when the grandparents died.'

'From the stress of looking after the children, no doubt,' said Pawley.

They stood astounded at their own moderation.

Though he had now retired, Gervaise still turned up at the next staff meeting. Who had the heart to turn him out, his empty pipe clenched between his teeth, unlit in compliance with the university policy of equal opportunity and non-smoking?

'I should like to propose a course on the early Conrad,' he said.

'I thought you were retired.'

'I am,' he said proudly, 'but that does not preclude me from offering a course.'

There was universal blinking and frowning.

'Unpaid, of course. This would be a donation to the department. To the common good. The terms of the package prohibit remuneration. But they specify quite clearly that an honorary associate shall be able to participate in the department's teaching and research program.'

'What a scab,' said Pawley.

'The man's a maniac,' said Lancaster. 'Who would ever teach who didn't have to?'

'Even many who have to don't,' said Dr Bee.

'Name of the game,' said Lancaster who'd just cancelled two weeks of his tutorials in order to attend a writers' conference in Manila.

'It's against every union principle,' said Pawley.

'Gervaise was ever in the front of political thought,' said Dr Bee. 'Now he's in the vanguard of union breaking.'

'We'll end up with all the courses taught for free by superannuated old shags,' said Pawley.

'Instead of being taught for money by the same old shags,' said Dr Bee.

'I thought the idea of early retirement was to provide openings for new staff,' said Henry.

'No it isn't,' said Pawley. 'As you very well know. The aim is to get rid of existing staff, not to appoint anyone new.'

'I suppose so,' Henry agreed. 'But this way we don't even get rid of Gervaise.'

'It's archetypal,' said Dr Bee. 'Early retirement is introduced. Suddenly there's a chance to get rid of Gervaise. Then he bamboozles them with his honorary associate scheme. The Head of Department leaps into it as a way of getting him off the books. Then he comes back with his umbrella and his briefcase and his foul smelling pipe into his honorary research associate's room and everything's the same as ever and he still takes up a parking space.'

'It's a scandal,' said Lancaster. 'Now Edwina and Gervaise are set here in perpetuity. Either they refuse to retire at retirement age and stay on, or they retire and come back as eternal associates and stay on. It's going to allow people like Gervaise to pick the eyes out of the courses, and the rest of us will end up teaching what's left.'

'It's appalling,' said Pawley. 'It just adds to the general climate of demoralisation and dissatisfaction.'

'Thought that would make you happy,' said Dr Bee.

15

Writing Class

Creative Writing had been Henry Lancaster's salvation. Sometimes as the day dawned and work loomed he would gaze across the bleak sea and remind himself how it could be worse, how it might have been worse, how it used to be worse. Teaching Literature. Every night the half-read novel, the incompleted epic. Some people read a book once in their life and remembered it. Not Lancaster. He did not want his head full of everything he'd ever read. He wanted space to conceive his own books. Sometimes it had seemed that he remembered nothing. And so week after week, year after year, he would be re-reading the texts he was teaching, and always the rush, the desperation, the incompletion.

So Creative Writing had been an idea of genius. For years he had scorned it. 'How can you teach writing?' he would ask. '*Poeta nascitur non fit.* Did I ever do a creative writing course?'

'Dangerous argument,' said Dr Bee. 'Maybe had you done one you wouldn't have been teaching literature now.'

'Either you have the talent or you don't,' said Lancaster.

But then an invitation to teach it in the States had altered his world view.

'It's a network,' said his London publisher. 'The teachers all know each other and pass their prettiest students around between them.'

That was in the days before the sexual harassment guidelines, the days when every successful student seduced its teacher. Anyway, Lancaster had been there, done that. What interested him now was a life of teaching without texts. Freedom from preparation. Now he had found the way to ensure the students did the preparation and he just listened.

'Right, who has something to read? Excellent. Off you go.'

And then, after the student had delivered, 'Excellent, well done. I enjoyed that. Comments? Anybody have any comments? What did you all think of that?'

It was like being a talk show host with compulsive celebrities, the ones who couldn't shut up, just let them go on and on.

The worst part was having to listen to what they read. It was something years of lecturing had made him ill suited for. But he learned. It was just a matter of sitting there and not falling asleep. Or sleeping lightly enough to hear when the reading stopped.

And at its best it was like the midday movies on television. Sit back, put your feet up, and switch on to the sequence of sex and horror, incest, abortion, family nightmares, drugs and desperation.

'Don't you sometimes worry that there might be a degree of voyeurism here?' asked Dr Bee.

'I am a camera,' said Lancaster.

'I see.'

'What is literature if not voyeurism? What are movies if not voyeurism? What is art if not voyeurism?'

'Well, quite a lot I've always thought,' said Dr Bee.

'Perhaps,' conceded Lancaster, magnanimously, magnificently. 'Perhaps there are some other things too. But there is always the voyeuristic core. How do other people live? What lies at the heart of being?'

'Tell me,' said Dr Bee.

'It is the question, not the answer,' said Lancaster. 'Always the question. We are always asking, we are always curious how other people live, that is the eternal impetus of writing,' said Lancaster.

'Is that so?' said Dr Bee.

But Lancaster was in unstoppable mode. He had spent two hours having to listen to his students read their stories, two hours without holding forth.

'Sometimes people ask, how can you teach creative writing?'

'I seem to remember you asking the same question,' said Dr Bee.

'My answer is, you don't, you can't teach creative writing,' said Lancaster. 'You provide the chance. The occasion. You encourage. You facilitate. You offer the window of opportunity.'

'I am a window cleaner, as it were,' said Dr Bee. 'Or rather, you are.'

'Exactly,' said Lancaster.

But it was not all exhilaration. Lancaster came in after one class his ashen, stricken self. It took a while before he spoke. Dr Bee waited affably.

'I just discovered one of my writing students is working as a call girl.'

'Have you got her number?' asked Dr Bee. 'Is she one of those who advertises in the classifieds?' He took a cutting out of his wallet. '"Candy and Roxy. Need help paying Uni fees. Visit us for a wild time. Satisfaction is guaranteed." I'd been meaning to give them a call. See if they were students of ours.'

'All grist to the media empires' mills,' said Pawley. 'Pumps up the small ads. The foundations of the global empire. Money from the child labour of paper boys and the immoral earnings of pimping for prostitution. The companies that pay tax at less than seven per cent.'

'I find it all a bit depressing,' said Henry.

'It's late capitalism.'

'I mean the call girl bit.'

'Same thing,' said Pawley. 'What else can you do with an arts degree in a post-industrial age?'

'His wife was prostitute to all the age, His pen was prostitute upon the stage,' said Dr Bee.

'It has a nice homology,' said Pawley, his eyes bloodshot pinpoints, catching the cosmic pattern of it. 'Henry sells his mind, she sells her body.'

'Is it your mind you sell, Henry?' asked Dr Bee. 'Or just your pen.'

'Ah, that's apt too,' said Pawley, 'the phallic pen, the –'

'Oh for heaven's sake,' Lancaster snapped.

'What else can you expect when they remove scholarships and introduce fees?' said Pawley. 'Capitalism. On what foundation is the present family, the bourgeois family based? On capital, on private gain. In its completely developed form this family exists only among the bourgeois. But this state of things finds its complement in the practical absence of the family among proletarians, and in public prostitution.'

'I bet you say that to all the girls,' said Dr Bee.

She had been waiting for him outside his room.

'I've got this manuscript I wondered if you'd read.'

'Just read it out in class,' Lancaster said, automatically evasive of undertaking to read anything.

'I'd rather not,' she said.

'Don't be nervous,' he said.

'I'm not nervous,' she said. 'It's just a bit, it might be a bit shocking.'

'I'm not easily shocked,' he said, Lancaster the shocker, the man of sensation.

'No, well,' she said, 'I took your advice.'

'My advice?' he said. It pleased him, though he couldn't think of any useful advice he'd given. What was there ever to say?

'When you said, don't think about it, just do it,' she said

'Ah, yes.'

'So I did it.'

'It was a whole manuscript about being on the game,' said Lancaster.

'Recognise any of the clients? Vice-Chancellor? Senior Management? Rowley?'

'I found it all rather, I don't know -'

'Voyeuristic, perhaps?' suggested Dr Bee.

'Depressing really,' said Lancaster.

'I'd have thought you'd have taken a more positive attitude,' said Dr Bee. 'Get her to fix you up with a couple of girls. Or a viewing booth. Ideal for the writer. A window on the world. You could probably pay out of your research funds. Think of it, Henry, the material, the sex, the opportunities. A new *Butterfield 8*. Or *The World of Suzie Wong*. You ought to be able to negotiate a percentage. That Japanese visiting professor who asked me to get him a girl, I'll tell him to give you a call. Maybe they could pay you a commission in kind so you didn't have to notify the university of other sources of income. Save you getting picked up for living off immoral earnings. Not that that seems to have worried them about your books.'

'How's the happy hooker?' asked Dr Bee.

Lancaster gave his pursed lip look, the British aesthete of the 1930s one.

'Manuscript all sealed and delivered? Film rights all fixed up?'

'It's so difficult,' said Lancaster.

It had been. How to tell her.

'It's good small press stuff,' he said. 'Literary magazines. But there aren't many small presses or literary magazines left. And you get a couple of hundred readers and that's it.'

How to say that if you want to go on record with memoirs of the sex trade, why not make some money out of it?

'The material's good. But you ought to make more of it. Market it. Make it more commercial.'

'I don't want to sell out,' she said.

'What do you mean?' asked Lancaster.

'I don't want to prostitute myself.'

'But isn't that what you're doing anyway?'

She laughed. 'I suppose it is. But writing's different.'

Who was he to deny that?

'So how do you go about getting published?' she asked.

He suggested she got to know publishers. Hung out round the literary scene. Book launches. Parties. Ingratiate yourself. Sidle up to the senior editors. How do you go about getting published, you go about it like getting into movies or television, on your back.

'Oh, but I couldn't do that.'

'What do you mean you couldn't do that?'

'That wouldn't be right.'

'But you do it all the time.'

'But I wouldn't feel right doing it to get published.'

He shook his head in dumb amazement.

'Think about it,' he said. He felt he'd already said too much. Was this the sort of advice expected of a writing teacher?

'You offered to show her round?' asked Dr Bee. 'Take her to the right places. Literary escort services?'

'Are you suggesting I should pimp my students?'

'Only the professionals,' said Dr Bee.

'She seemed resistant,' said Lancaster. 'She tells me one of the girls she works with did a deal with her dentist. Got her teeth fixed for you know, as she put it, rather than cash. But writing, she seems to have this elevated idea of it.'

'Can't imagine where she'd have learned that from,' said Dr Bee.

The Head of Department arrived for her morning tea and chocolate biscuits. Dr Bee sought clarification.

'What do the sexual guidelines say about having sex with a student who earns her living as a prostitute? Or his or her living, to be non-gender specific. What if you went to a brothel or phoned up an agency and you found it was one of your students you were offered? What would the official university ruling be about that? Should you, could you, go ahead? Or should you withdraw, as it were?'

'I think you should put it down in writing and make a formal submission,' said the Head of Department.

'In writing,' mused Dr Bee.

'Or is it too urgent?'

16

Lunch

Pawley, Henry Lancaster and Dr Bee took to going off campus for lunch. It was the faculty club's introduction of access by electronic smart card that Pawley objected to.

'They did it at the White House,' he said. 'All the journalists freaked. It isn't just that it electronically lets you in. It's not just to cut down on staff by sacking the doorman.'

'There never was a doorman as far as I can recall,' said Dr Bee. 'Never a club you could really call a club. I'd be happy to go somewhere decent.'

'It's for control,' Pawley went on. 'It records who goes in when. Who's in high security areas and how often.'

'I hardly see the faculty club as a high security area,' said Dr Bee.

'It's all a matter of monitoring. Who goes to lunch early every day. Who goes in for an evening drink. How long they stay.'

'But you don't use the card to leave,' said Dr Bee.

'An oversight,' said Pawley.

It wasn't just the smart card. That may have prompted Pawley to action, but Henry's pre-ulcer and gall bladder and gout were playing up. He was anxious about everything he ate. Ever since the old Asia hand had keeled over at the Thanksgiving lunch he'd been uneasy.

'You assured me it was before he'd eaten the lunch,' said Dr Bee. 'He was still in the queue. Probably died of hunger from waiting.'

'The most lethal viruses and poisons are inhaled,' said Pawley. 'Don't need to ingest them. Just breathe them in. Sniff it up with the smell of the gravy and it's snuffed you out. Like anthrax. Or Mad Cow Disease. It's known in the trade as neurosurgeon's disease.'

'Known in which trade?' asked Dr Bee.

'Neurosurgery,' said Pawley. 'They inhale it doing brain operations. It's not even the case you have to eat the brains like an anthropologist at a cannibal's feast.'

'Please,' said Henry. 'No more. I feel sick already.'

'Reminds you of your travels?' said Dr Bee. 'What did they serve you at that Pan-African Congress of Committed Writers? You should be grateful for Pawley's researches. As you always say, everything is food to the novelist's imagination. A novel on Mad Cow Disease would seem very apposite to our present situation. Does it infect bulls to, or is it exclusively a disease of equal opportunity?'

As for Dr Bee, he announced his refusal to encounter the Dead Hand, Deadwood Edwina or the Head of Department on any further occasion.

'I've already stopped going to staff meetings so as not to deal with them. Now they plague my lunch time. Paralyse the colon just by their presence.'

Pawley agreed. 'Brings you down, I agree. It takes me three

or four joints to get back to normal temperature and pulse rate after an encounter with them. Costs me a fortune. I don't need it. I want a relaxing lunch, a quiet smoke on the way, some small meat-free entrée and a good desert.'

'Déjeuner de l'herbe,' said Dr Bee.

On top of which was the problem of the barman. He had become too friendly.

'Barmen are always hit-men or informers in the movies,' said Pawley.

'Or both,' agreed Dr Bee.

They would only have to walk through the door and he would have their regular order poured: Lancaster's red wine, Dr Bee's gin and tonic, Pawley's low alcohol beer. It was flattering for a while. And the club was dying like everything else on campus. Not too many people went in there any more. It probably wasn't hard to remember the regulars and what they drank.

'Especially if you're trained,' said Pawley. 'So you know who to slip a Mickey Finn to.'

And if the barman noticed, who else noticed? Were the regulars from administration also recording everything? Was it all being reported?

'I always remember the old Deputy Vice-Chancellor coming up to me one night,' Henry recalled. '"We have our ways of knowing if someone's drinking too much," he said, "or if they're playing around." I never knew if it was a personal warning or just his usual self-aggrandising megalomania.'

'Were you, then?' asked Dr Bee.

'Was I what?'

'Drinking too much and playing around.'

'Ah, the heady sixties,' said Lancaster. 'All for the novel, mind you. Field work. Bliss was it in that dawn to be alive.'

'Which one was Dawn?' asked Dr Bee.

It was too convenient to drink at the club. And in a context of global inconvenience, convenience in the post-modern university suggested entrapment, some sort of administration sting.

Pawley looked at the newly lowered ceiling. Supposedly to make the club more friendly.

'Makes us feel we stand taller. Closer to the light fittings,' said Lancaster.

'Personally it makes me feel I'm walled up in the catacombs,' said Dr Bee.

'It's to accommodate listening devices,' Pawley said. 'Monitor subversion. It's the obvious place. A lot of the work's sensitive. Genetic engineering. Germ warfare. Political Science. Anthropology. Asian Studies. It's all about counter-insurgency and the war against terrorism and chemical weapons and manipulating electoral processes. They need to monitor people working on this stuff. Check their loyalties. Who they're telling what to.'

'And this they?' said Dr Bee.

'Ah,' said Pawley, 'as Rousseau lamented, if only I knew who was behind it all. The stasi. Internal security. Let alone the university's own security service. If indeed it is an independent service.'

'You make it sound quite exciting,' said Henry. 'Never imagined there was so much going on. Never imagined there was anything going on, to be honest.'

'The failure of the imagination,' said Pawley. 'Think of all those visiting writers you bring here for a drink. They're all either oppositional subversives or government agents in their own countries.'

'Probably both,' agreed Dr Bee.

'They'd all be under surveillance. And multiply that by all the other people who bring in guests. There's quite a lot to watch.'

'If only there were,' said Dr Bee, gazing at the ranks of empty chairs.

Overdetermined their decision may have been. But it was a decision amidst the vast prevarication. An escape from the prison camp. And they didn't have to dig a tunnel, conceal the earth, trowel away underground every night. They just drove through the gates. Not even in a laundry van. A delirious sense of truancy. No one counting the number of glasses any longer. Or bottles for that matter.

'Lunch,' said Henry, 'should be sacred. A little eternity between twelve and three.' He held his glass of retsina to the light, recalling happy days in the isles of Greece, the isles of Greece, Ritsos, Cavafy, Kazantzakis, long languorous lunches, longer more languorous dinners.

'We have a civilising mission in this dark continent,' he said. 'Weaning the ignorant millions from their horrid ways. Inculcate a respect for the finer things of life. Civilised discourse. Teaching should be prohibited from twelve till three. Absolutely indecent that people teach all through the lunch hour. How can the students learn anything? If they don't have time to sit and talk in the Union when will they ever talk? They don't learn from us. They learn from talking things through amongst themselves. And as for us, how can we teach if we're on the go all the time? The batteries run down. The well dries up.'

Dr Bee poured him another drink and went back to watching the waitress.

'Damn it,' Henry continued. 'A man's got to eat. And in a civilised way. All these body bag lunches, absolutely vile. No wonder the quality's gone. What sort of work can you expect from people who sit in their offices eating refrigerated sandwiches out of paper bags and drinking out of plastic bottles and polystyrene cups? On their own. That's what they do.'

It was true. That was what they did. From eleven-thirty onwards there would be a steady stream of staff shuffling across to the Union and returning with their brown paper bags and bottle of mineral water or cup of decaffeinated coffee.

'Or spend all their lunch time in meetings,' he went on. 'That's another outrage. Time-tabling lunch-time departmental meetings.'

'You want breakfast ones like American business?' said Pawley, stubbing out his roll-your-own in the ash-tray, a restaurant where ash-trays were still provided, the rebetika tape potentiating the hashish, the hashish potentiating the appetite, the tzatziki and taramasalata and dolmades and Kalamata olives winking there in the Attic light.

'I don't want meetings at all,' said Henry. 'Never seen the point of them. They're like the parliament of Hell. Everything's always been fixed up beforehand. And I certainly refuse to attend them at mealtimes ever again.'

He poured himself another glass, Dr Bee distracted.

'Might need to order another bottle now,' Henry continued. 'Otherwise we'll get too anxious worrying about whether there'll be enough to see us through the main course. No point in getting anxious. Causes heart disease. Affects the immune system. Raises the cholesterol level. No, we have to watch our health. No more stress. No more departmental meetings. A proper respect for appointed meal times.' He tapped Dr Bee on the upper arm to attract his attention. 'Call the waitress over and I'll order another bottle,' he said. 'Should have done this years ago. All those dreadful lunchtimes with the Dead Hand.' He shuddered. 'What a waste. Still –.' He drained his glass and chewed on an olive till the next bottle arrived.

It gave them a new interest in life. The pleasures of research. The thrill of discovery. The connoisseurship of taste. They sampled the various restaurants that were not too far from the university, places they could drive to easily and get back from for an afternoon class, yet not so close as to be contaminated by its ambience. Once in a while they struck a dud: some hidden little sea-food dive Gervaise had recommended, a nouvelle cuisine atrocity where one of Dr Bee's students was serving. But soon they had established their preferred spots. They stuck to them.

They were in the Golden Bowl, a quiet little Italian number tucked away in the inner city. Dr Bee insisted on sitting at a table in the window so he could watch the girls mincing around the boutique across the road.

'Stimulates the juices,' he said.

Lancaster looked across jadedly. 'Much like the university,' he said. 'They stand at the door and no one comes.'

No one had been to his classes all week. It had been essay week. Hand in assignments week.

'It's not that I'm that unpopular,' he said. 'Surely.'

'Nothing to do with it,' said Dr Bee. 'With all the assignments due this week they wouldn't have come even if you weren't.'

'Control again,' said Pawley. 'Control versus education. The priorities are compulsory handing in of written work, with a penalty rate of ten per cent deduction from the mark for every day late. What a travesty. No onc carcs that as a result no one comes to class. Education, who cares? Literature, who cares? All that matters is getting the work in on time.'

Across the road one of the graffiti proclaimed 'Liberals = Mussolini.'

'I can never decide whether that's meant as an encouragement to vote Liberal or the opposite,' mused Lancaster.

'It was one of those lies introduced in the sixties and seventies,' said Pawley.

'What was?' asked Lancaster.

'Continuous assessment. A bondage under the guise of progressive reform. The students complained about the tyranny of examinations at the end of the year, so they were given essays and assignments all through the year. It killed the student magazines and theatre let alone politics. No one can afford the time off to write or act.'

'In my day you could take a whole term off to write a novel or edit a magazine,' said Lancaster. 'I certainly did.'

'You still do,' said Dr Bee.

'It's the only way,' said Lancaster. 'How else will we maintain the culture?'

'But students can't do that any more,' said Pawley. 'Assessing them by continual essays and assignments was a way of keeping their noses to the grindstone. Stopped them demonstrating, stopped them thinking.'

'Their noses,' said Dr Bee. 'What about our noses? We're the ones who have to do all the marking throughout the year.'

'Exactly,' said Pawley. 'I used to think it was just a control on the students. Now I realise it was to control us, to keep us endlessly marking. All through the semester after the mid-semester break. All through the break between the semesters. In the past you could use the vacations to write something, read something, to think about the subject. But that's all been stopped. Now it's endless marking. They've turned the university into a high school. They don't want an intelligentsia. It's not just that they want uneducated graduates who'll go happily into unemployment and ask no questions about the system. They don't want an intelligentsia formulating any questions about the system either.'

They looked across at the girls in the boutique. They felt a kindred feeling with them. Their own university rooms may not have been as elegant, their masculine forms not as young and lithe; they were less ready to walk around and prance and posture and gesture and move and bow and stretch. But they had one thing in common in the deep recession of the times. A lack of patronage, a failure of custom.

It was the last unviolated moment of their escape.

The light Italian white wine, recalling past idylls, conferences in Florence, residencies in Bellagio, death in Venice; the girls in the boutique like hieroglyphs on Egyptian tombs; Pawley's hash-laden joint stubbed out in the ash tray, all the varied colours of the antipasto vibrant before them, egg plant, capsicum, zucchini, sun-dried tomato, mushroom.

And then one of the Head of Department's protegés, Pamela, or was it Clarissa, some eager, spiky, post-graduate anyway, went by on the pavement. And turned. Smiled at them knowingly through the window.

They were chilled to the marrow.

'How did she know to look round and see us in the corner?' asked Pawley.

'You think at other inner city restaurants there might be other graduate students on patrol, looking for truant senior staff?' said Dr Bee.

'Wouldn't be surprised,' said Henry. 'Better order another bottle. This may be our last supper.'

Could the Head of Department really have organised patrols? Could Edwina have instructed the university security service? Or was it a direct action group of postgraduates manipulated by some CIA funded national student body?

'We won't tell,' said a particularly distasteful, ingratiating, shaven-headed, lip and navel-pierced, tongue-studded post-graduate who spoke to them in a pub bistro a couple of days later, grinning as it and its distasteful partner passed their table.

At the North Indian diner the following week their worst fears were confirmed.

Amidst their plates of dhal and koofta, of paneer saag and chana, with the fresh nan and the mango and lime chutneys, Ms Chung found them.

She bore down on them smiling.

'Well, well,' she said.

In the past they might have said, take a seat. But not in these harassment tribunal days.

'So this is where you all hang out.'

Lancaster laughed nervously and non-communicatively.

'Plotting?' she said.

Pawley sipped at his lassi, the only lassi he dared touch these days.

'Or just wagging school?'

'Up to a point,' said Lancaster.

'What price my silence?' she asked enigmatically, and walked out. Slowly.

'I'm afraid we know what price,' said Lancaster.

'Ah well,' said Dr Bee, 'sometimes a chap has to surrender himself for the well-being of his fellows. A man's got to do what a man's got to do.'

He rose from the table.

'I am just going outside and may be some time,' he said.

17

Research Assistants

Once again it was grant grabbing time. Once again those who had received thousands of dollars received thousands of dollars more. No matter that nothing ever resulted. No matter that nothing was ever published. Those who had proved their worth by receiving grants now had their worth rewarded by receiving more grants. All the senior academic management received grants. No matter that they spent every day on committees, reviewing other universities, representing professional associations, assessing grant applications. No one saw fit to inquire how they would do the research. After all they were administrators. They had received their promotion through administrative skills. They were above the daily toil of reading books. They spent no time in the libraries. They scribbled down no thoughts. The grants brought largesse and the largesse bought research assistants and so the projects were run, by people so busy and elevated and endlessly caballing and committeeing that there was no fear that they would need to contribute any input and little danger that anything would result. The faculty met and congratulated its deans and pro-deans and deputy chairs of this and that on receiving public funding, and all the people with nothing better to do than attend faculty meetings, those with no drive to read or write or think or research, applauded each other in the grand degeneration of the times.

'We should think of a project,' said Henry over lunch. 'Make ourselves less marginal. Something that need never result in anything. Something that would involve endless travel. Teams of research assistants. Something to bring in the money. Then we would be valued.'

'You think?' said Dr Bee.

'We will never be valued,' said Pawley. 'We're next in line now. Now Robert and Gervaise have gone, we're in the sights.'

'But if we landed a massive grant?' said Henry.

'We wouldn't,' said Pawley. 'The same people who want to get rid of us give out the grants. They are the assessors.'

'Not exactly,' said Henry.

'Close enough,' said Pawley.

'That's too paranoid,' said Henry.

'Nothing is too paranoid,' said Pawley.

'We could go to industry,' said Henry. 'Get industry to subsidise us.'

'The only industry we've had any connection with is the publishing industry and we subsidise it,' said Pawley. 'We provide the cheap product which it exploits. We ask for nothing. We're so eager to get into print so we can put something on our publications report that we let them pay us nothing.'

Henry snuffled and grunted. He was torn between embittered agreement and the need to conceal from himself and others the years of bad contracts, exploitation, humiliation.

It was a cold, grey day. Drizzle drifted across the street. Henry gazed at the pub opposite.

'What goes on in those upstairs rooms of pubs?' he asked. 'Have you ever been upstairs in a pub? There are all those rooms and all these years I've never been in one. I imagine it would be cold and bare and gray, linoleum floors, a wash basin, it would be a vision of cold, gray despair.'

'Today is a vision of cold, gray despair,' said Dr Bee. 'Why imagine upstairs rooms in a pub? Just look at the world around us. Just go into your upstairs room in the university.'

'My word,' said Henry. It was afternoon tea and he seemed remarkably cheered.

'Which one?' asked Dr Bee. 'You have written so many.'

'Ah-ha, my short friend,' said Henry, 'brevity is the soul of wit, what? You obviously haven't seen what my eyes have seen or you wouldn't be so grumpy.'

'The coming of the lord?' asked Dr Bee.

'Not at all. More like the scarlet woman.'

'Oh, the whore of Babylon.'

'That beautiful creature in the room next door to Rowley.'

'Yes. His research assistant.'

'His what?' said Henry.

'His research assistant. If you spent less time at airports and writers' festivals you could have been slavering for months. She's been here ever since he got back. Before he went away again.'

'You can't be serious.'

'I can be,' said Dr Bee, 'and I am.'

'What an outrage,' said Henry. 'What does he want a research assistant for?'

'From the look of her I'd have thought the answer would have been obvious.'

'But he never does any research. He never does anything except go away.'

'He may be tempted to do certain things now.'

'I can't believe it,' said Henry. 'It's beyond words.'

'Bury your grief and write a novel about it,' said Dr Bee.

'It's beyond fiction.'

'That's never stopped you in the past.'

It tormented Henry. He went down the corridor to take another look.

'You know why the great nineteenth-century novelists wrote so many books,' said Henry.

'They had talent?' suggested Dr Bee.

'They worked hard?' suggested Pawley.

'They had servants,' said Henry.

'Ah,' said Dr Bee. 'As for writing, our servants will do that for us.'

'For heaven's sake,' said Henry. 'The servants didn't write. They gave the novelists time by doing all the things that stop us from writing.'

'Going to airports, having lunch, getting pissed?' said Pawley.

'Shopping, cooking, cleaning, dusting, washing, all the daily domestic trivia,' said Henry.

'The rich texture of lived experience, I think you mean,' said Dr Bee.

'It's all so time consuming,' Henry wailed. 'I spent two hours this morning at the supermarket.'

'I rather enjoy it,' said Dr Bee. 'Following bored housewives around the aisles. Rubbing trolleys with them. Sharing their illicit desires at the chocolate shelves. I'd have thought it would have provided a fund of material for a novelist. The way we live now.'

'I hate it,' said Henry.

'Get yourself a research assistant,' suggested Pawley.

'What, to do the shopping?'

'Rowley does,' said Pawley. 'I saw her down at the bottle shop choosing his wine.'

'I don't believe it for a moment,' said Henry. 'When did you ever go to a bottle shop you lying tea-head?

'Now that's a word I haven't heard for a while,' said Dr Bee. 'Are you writing a historical romance, or has your mastery of contemporary idiom faltered?'

'Dope drought,' said Pawley. 'Dealer got busted. Had to find a substitute substance to abuse.'

'You're not serious?' said Henry.

'Sure am,' said Pawley. 'Had to go to court as a character witness for him.'

'About Rowley's research assistant,' Henry persisted.

'Absolutely,' said Pawley. 'What else would he use her for?'

Dr Bee gave a sinister stage laugh.

'He never does any research.'

'He's not alone in that,' said Pawley.

'I thought the whole point of a research assistant was just that anyway,' said Dr Bee. 'To spare you from having to do any research. You get your assistant to do all the work and just put your name to it when it's done.'

'Like having children,' said Pawley. 'From the man's point of view, that is.'

'Might be worth looking into, Henry,' said Dr Bee. 'A way to get your novels written.'

'You may laugh,' said Henry.

'It's all that's left to us,' said Dr Bee.

'You may laugh, but I've met novelists in the States with research assistants. "What do they actually do?" I asked. And apart from providing the usual sexual favours, they did things like look up which model of automobile was current in 1947 or what the weather was in Minnesota in July 1952, or what were the hit records of 1956.'

'All the sensuous fabric of the American way of life,' said Dr Bee.

'Seemed a scandal to me,' said Henry.

'And not an appealing one?'

'Not at all,' he said. 'Not at all.' But he sounded unconvincing, even to himself. The sight of Rowley's scarlet woman had unsettled him. It had started him thinking. Silently, subconsciously, like conceiving a novel, a seed had been planted and was slowly preparing to germinate.

'When I first joined the department,' said Dr Bee, 'I used to drink at the pub across the road with the psychologists. What a beautiful brood they were. All into Reich and orgone energy.'

He closed his eyes momentarily and the happy afternoons flooded back.

'Some of the rat-runners had research assistants who drank over there. They would spend every afternoon in the pub. The research assistants. I asked them when they did their rat-running. And it turned out they never did. They knew the results that were wanted, and they just provided them.'

'What, faked them?' said Henry.

'Well, that's one way of putting it. They had no compunctions. The alternative would have been to have kept on running the experiments till they got the results that were wanted. So rather than waste time and energy they just provided the results straight away.'

'So the whole scientific edifice of modern society is built on fraud,' said Henry.

'I would have thought so, yes,' said Dr Bee.

'Like the IQ tests in Britain,' said Pawley. 'The ones they used to justify the segregating of schoolchildren at age eleven into grammar schools or secondary moderns. All that data was faked. It created a caste society for forty years. All on the basis of fraud.'

'You would have preferred to create a caste society on the

basis of truth?' asked Dr Bee.

'There is no scientific truth,' said Pawley. 'It's all a matter of creating some fraudulent mystification as a basis for ruling class ideology.'

'And what ruling class ideology is Rowley's research assistant propping up?' asked Dr Bee.

'I intend to find out,' said Henry.

Henry began his own research. He bailed her up at afternoon tea. Rowley was overseas at King's or Queen's or Duke or Lords.

'Did he leave you work to do? Or are you in instant e-mail communication?'

'What people don't understand,' she said, 'is that he doesn't give me work to do. I generate my own work.'

'Ah,' said Henry.

Dialogue, dialogue, he smelled self-delusive dialogue, the very stuff of fiction.

'So what are you generating?'

'I'm generating a bibliography,' she said. 'Then I abstract the material that I think he should read.'

'And does he?'

'Does he what?'

'Does he read it?'

She delivered her haughtiest 'Of course.'

'And what happens then?'

'What happens then?'

'Yes, what happens when he reads what you give him?'

She gathered herself up and left, all scarlet fingernails and lipstick.

'I think you should ask the professor himself,' she said.

Research assistants were now the name of the game.

'Who are these people?' Henry would ask as a fresh troop of

new hirelings left the common room.

'Oh, they're research assistants.'

For the Dead Hand, the Head of Department, Gervaise, Rowley, Philippa and the rest.

No matter that no research was published. Those with grants hired research assistants. It was the modern mark of academic status. Having a grant. Having a servant.

Applying for a grant was a time-consuming business.

'It took me a month to fill in the forms and write the project proposal,' said Pawley.

'So it should,' said the Head of Department. She was a member of the grant giving committee. 'It's a serious business,' she said.

It certainly was. So serious that Pawley was refused one. Maybe the committee baulked at several kilos of consumable research materials. Maybe the topic of 'Hashish and the Literary Imagination' with itemised travel expenses to Morocco and Jamaica was not sufficiently politically correct.

'You should have called it "Mary Jane and the feminine literary imagination,"' said Dr Bee. 'Or "When one is tired of life what is left but boys and hashish? Bhang and Buggery in the writing of the Decadents."'

'It's not the faking I mind,' said Dr Bee. 'It's all these reverend caterpillars poncing around as team leaders of research projects their assistants are doing for them. Claiming vast expertise. People too busy at committees to do their research hiring a team of research assistants paid for by the tax-payer to provide them with material to ensure their promotion to higher positions from which they can hire even more research assistants.

'And on the rare occasions their research assistants do produce a book for them,' Dr Bee went on, 'they put their own name to it and keep the royalties. They hire research assistants at the tax-payers' expense who write the book and then they copyright the books in their own name, or in their wife's name or some company name to avoid tax, and take all the royalties.'

'You want to return the royalties to the state?' asked Henry. 'I never heard you support the state before.'

Dr Bee just grunted.

'At least those scoundrels produce something,' said Henry. He always had a notional soft spot for the idea of fellow authors, even if the books were ghost written, even if he didn't get on so well with fellow authors in the flesh. 'But what about the old God professors who've had research assistants on departmental funds for thirty years and never produced anything? Shouldn't the cost to the tax-payer be deducted from their pensions when they retire? Or taken out of their estate when they die?'

Idle fantasies of punitive measures for rainy afternoons. While Rowley toured the world, attaching himself to research institutes in the isles of Greece, Uttar Pradesh, Ultima Thule, the Outer Hesperides.

'How could you trust anybody else to do the work for you?' asked Pawley.

'I thought your dope intake had ensured you never trusted anybody for anything,' said Dr Bee.

'Dope doesn't make you paranoid,' said Pawley, passing the joint across. 'It just opens your eyes.'

'I see,' said Dr Bee, exhaling slowly.

'How could you be sure a research assistant had been thorough or accurate, let alone honest? And what of serendipity?'

'What indeed?' said Dr Bee, taking another drag.

'You know when you're working through the library stacks looking for a book and your eye catches a title on another shelf, some book you didn't know existed that turns out to be relevant to what you're looking for. Or when you're scanning through a journal for an article you notice another piece on a different topic and you find it's spot on for what you're working on. But would a research assistant hired to look for specific items be open to these chances in the same way? Would a research assistant know enough to know what was relevant, to see the pattern in the peripheral? You've got to be in tune with the cosmic flow, you've got to be open to the random, to synchronicity.'

'You've got to be stoned,' glossed Dr Bee.

'Absolutely,' said Pawley.

'Doesn't seem to be a problem for you,' said Dr Bee. 'So what made you apply for a grant?'

'Greed,' said Pawley. 'Sheer grasping greed and base competitiveness. Everyone else had one so why shouldn't I? What a bad idea. Glad I got knocked back. Having a research assistant is just having a spy in your office as far as I can see. A merciful escape. Much better to get on with your work in your own way.'

'Stoned?' said Dr Bee.

'Absolutely,' agreed Pawley, rolling another one.

'What's this then?' asked Henry.

Rowley's assistant was sitting at morning tea with a slim volume in front of her. Henry reached across and picked it up. *The Grand Tour: a Guide.*

'What, Rowley's actually written a book? I can't believe it.'

'Nor can I,' said the research assistant.

'Well if you can't believe it, who can?' said Henry.

'I can't believe he'd do this to me.'

The gentleman emerged in Henry, the damp shoulder ever receptive to a weeping female.

'Tell me,' he said, all his literary charm, all his luring of confidences at work.

He picked it up and leafed through it.

'Oh, it's a bibliography. I thought it was a travel book from the title. Should sell a few hundred to the unsuspecting.'

'Of course it's a bibliography,' she said. 'I compiled it for him. And he doesn't even acknowledge me. Not even so much as mention me. I compiled the whole thing. I did it all. I sent it to him and he didn't even change an entry. Not a word. Except to put his own name on it and publish it as his.'

'He probably forgot you actually existed,' said Henry, all care and consideration. 'Probably thought you were one of those research assistants he'd invented in order to claim their salaries.'

'I slaved over this,' she said, her fingernails blood red. 'And I don't think he even looked at it. He's not added anything. He's not even changed anything. It's exactly as I gave it him on disk. Wouldn't you have thought he'd at least have thanked me?'

'Indeed I would,' said Henry. It was a lie, nothing too base could be thought of Rowley in his experience. But he added more truthfully, or at least more compassionately, 'I would indeed, had it been me.'

'I'm through,' she said. 'I'm resigning. I'm outraged.'

'What will you do?' asked Henry.

'There are other jobs,' she said. 'I don't need this sort of treatment. I'll find someone who respects my work.'

'Absolutely,' said Henry. 'Look, it's nearly lunch time. What say we go out for a bite to eat? There's a little project I'd like to talk to you about. Well, not that little actually. I might have access to some research funds and -'

He let it hang there. Alluringly, he hoped.

'I have to clock up another three hours.'

'Charge it to Rowley,' said Henry. 'Give lunch an added piquancy. Paid for on Rowley's time. Make up for all the credit he never gave you. Steal a bit of it back.'

She looked at him warily for a moment, and then the book caught her eye again.

'Why not?' she said.

18

I am Available

Dr Bee sat mournfully in the common room, gazing at a colour polaroid in his hand.

'Sort of thing they used to sell in Port Said in my day,' said Gervaise, peering over his shoulder.

'You must show me your collection some time,' said Dr Bee.

'Out on the boat,' said Gervaise, disregarding the familiar waspishness. 'Row out one weekend and flick through them over a drink.'

'When the sun's passed over the yard arm?'

'Something like that,' said Gervaise. 'Earlier if you like.'

He eased himself into his chair, his arthritic knees rusty from the salt air.

'Take it yourself?' he asked, nodding at the photograph.

'It was attached to a student's late essay,' said Dr Bee.

Gervaise peered at it more closely. 'Funny sort of medical certificate. No signs of the pox or anything. Usually they're telling you how sick they are so they couldn't submit on time.'

'I think the point she's making is that she is willing to submit at any time,' said Dr Bee. He turned the photograph over. On the back was written 'I am available.'

'I'd be careful if I were you,' said Gervaise. 'Might find her husband waiting in the next room to beat you up. Remember when poor old Rowley went a-wooing in the Campus Motel? Caught in flagrante by somebody's boyfriend. He tried calling out for help. "I am being attacked in two hundred and seven." People just assumed it was some group sex multiple of soixante-neuf. Made a frightful mess of him. Got into the papers. Those were the days.'

Dr Bee sighed and put the photograph back into his wallet.

'Seem to have quite a wad of them there,' said Gervaise.

'I'll show you mine when you show me yours,' said Dr Bee.

'It's not the job it was,' said Gervaise. 'I can remember the days when girls would turn up wearing nothing but a trenchcoat, knock on your door, and bare all before you. There for the taking. Never thought anything of it. But now. . . . All this harassment nonsense. Could all be out on our ears tomorrow. That's why I keep the boat. Never know when you may have to up anchor and sail away.'

They brooded in mutual gloom.

'Let's have another look at that lass,' said Gervaise. 'Cheer up an old fellow's heart before he goes out to the front line again.'

Dr. Bee took out his wallet and obliged.

'Where the bee sucks, there suck I,' murmured Gervaise, mindful of the long s's in the long grass. 'Though I think one should still be careful,' he added. 'Never know. Could be blackmail. Might find oneself kidnapped and sold into white slavery. Or chopped up for body parts. Never know these days.'

'I am all things to all men,' said Ms Chung. 'And to all women too. A goulash of racial genes. A smorgasbord of ethnicity.'

Dr Bee felt he was slavering. He could feel his taste buds stimulated, the saliva flowing.

'But first,' she said, 'we do some business. In my country it is a disgrace to return without a degree.'

'What country is your country?' he asked.

She waved her hand airily, sinuously.

'I am a citizen of the world,' she said. 'But I must have a degree. If I fail my courses, I will be discredited. There will be nothing left but to kill you and then kill the Head of Department.'

'Well, start with the Head of Department, you know, ladies first in our country.'

'I could be your mail-order bride,' said Ms Chung.

'I've already got a bride.'

'Get rid of her.'

'She mightn't like that. And I'd probably end up losing the house and car like Gervaise.'

'Demote her,' said Ms Chung. 'In my country a man can have four wives.'

'They obviously arrange things better in your country,' said Dr Bee.

'We fly there in the vacation and make the arrangements,' said Ms Chung. 'After I receive my degree, huh?'

It was the Head of Department who first broke the news. She had called on Dr Bee at his home. It was a matter of double-marking some examination papers and the only way to speed up things was to deliver a batch of scripts in her four-wheel drive.

Mrs Bee answered the door.

'Oh come in,' she said. 'He's in bed with his mistress. He won't be long. He never is. Just take a seat.'

The Head of Department took a seat while Mrs Bee carried on with the vacuum cleaner.

Dr Bee emerged in his bathrobe like a Roman emperor or a Japanese wrestler, wreathed with a cherubic smile of self-satisfaction. He handed over the papers.

'Like a drink or something?' he asked.

The Head of Department declined. She found the situation uneasy, Mrs Bee hoovering round the skirting boards behind her.

Ms Chung slid through the bedroom door in an oriental dressing gown adorned with dragons and peacocks.

'And then what happened?' said Gervaise. 'Tell us more. Did they invite you in with them?'

'He's supposed to have a heart condition,' said the Head of Department. 'He gave me a letter from his doctor saying he shouldn't be required to attend staff meetings because it was a strain on his heart and blood pressure.'

Philippa reached out a calming hand, patted her on the arm.

'Don't let him provoke you,' she said. 'We don't want you ending up with the heart attack.'

'Don't know about that,' muttered Gervaise.

Then Gervaise reported a sighting Saturday midnight in the department.

'Just bumped into them in the corridor, wrapped all round him like the proverbial serpent.'

'What were you doing in the department corridor at midnight on a Saturday?' asked Lancaster. 'Staking them out?'

'Not at all. Just popped up to the heads to clean the teeth. Rinsing the old molars ready for the nightly grind. I'd've offered them my old couch but the wife and the lawyers took it. Didn't feel I could offer them the hammock. Bit risky in my experience.'

The news went round.

'He probably staged it just to discommode the Head of Department,' said Lancaster.

'You can't accept it might be true?' said Gervaise. 'Ah, the limitations of the imagination. Truth is stranger than fiction. You ought to know that. That's why nobody reads novels any more. You should take up biography.'

It kept them all speculating. What was Dr Bee's fatal charm? How did his wife accept it? How did he keep the balance? But he did. The three of them would all turn up for a drink in the evening at the faculty club, Dr Bee sitting like some travelling potentate in western clothes, wife and mistress on each side of him.

It was even more effective than mentioning a book for driving out the Dead Hand. It affronted all his code of negations and denials. He would make for the door as soon as the trio appeared.

Gervaise would stand at the bar prognosticating doom and gloom.

'He'll pay for it,' he said. 'My word, he'll pay for it. I lost everything and I only had one woman. They'll take him for everything and a mortgage on the next life too.'

Dr Bee only beamed, as the days passed on in their gentle way, and rocked the tedious year as in a delightful dream.

But in Lancaster's analysis it was a major contribution to the escalating demoralisation of the department. It undercut all the certainties by its very openness. The public proclamation of wife and mistress, the mutual acceptances, destabilised all the other uneasy, uncertain relationships.

'It's even made the Dead Hand anxious. You can see him thinking, "Why not me?" I sometimes wonder if it isn't primarily a psychological warfare exercise. Just to undermine us all.'

'You can't accept it might just be libido and they're all enjoying themselves,' said Pawley.

'No,' said Lancaster. 'That would be too awful. No, I think

it's far more likely he's in league with the Vice-Chancellor and the Ministry. Part of the campaign to destabilise us. Make us desperate and dissatisfied so we'll take early retirement.'

Lancaster came into the common room one afternoon just as Dr Bee was leaving.

'Sorry I can't stop,' said Dr Bee. 'Have to see someone. I'm thinking of getting a girlfriend. Keep it to yourself, mind you. I wouldn't want it getting out. Could make things a bit tricky on the domestic fronts.'

Lancaster hammered on Pawley's door.

'It has to be psychological warfare. He's trying to destroy our spirit. Otherwise he wouldn't have told me. He knows you never tell a writer anything in confidence. It's like saying "off the record" to a journalist.'

Pawley lit a joint and passed it across.

'Here, have a smoke and calm down.'

Lancaster reached out with shaking hand.

'Then you can face the worst.'

'What worst?'

Pawley beckoned him over to the window. They stood there and watched Dr Bee opening his car door for Rowley's research assistant to step inside.

19

Down-sizing and Multi-skilling

Inexorably the feminisation of the department continued. Reclaim the night, and then put out the lights.

'All future appointments will have to be women,' the Head of Department proclaimed.

'Doesn't that contravene union policy?' asked Gervaise, who'd been a rabid anti-union man all his life.

'No,' said the Head of Department confidently.

'Is that what is meant by equality of opportunity?'

'Yes.'

'And cultural diversity?'

But it was not only a matter of the new appointments. There were so few of them, anyway. It was the promotion ladder. Two by two the women climbed effortlessly up the scale. The men got nowhere. They floundered on the shore, drowning as the waters of purgation engulfed them.

'Why stay?' the naiads whispered to them. 'Why suffer a slow lingering death? Why not just get up and go? There is no future for you here.'

Robert had been the first to crack and pack it in. Years of destabilisation had made him an easy target. And once one had gone, the pressure built up. The Head of Department sensed she was on a winning streak. Downsizing. The men began to crumble. Gervaise took the package.

'It will be George Hill next,' said Dr Bee. 'He went wild boar shooting with Gervaise last weekend. He's obviously keeping his hand in for something big.'

'Multiskilling. That's the name of the game in this era of downsizing,' said Henry.

'I thought the name of the game was coining the neologisms that rule our lives,' said Pawley.

'Looked into that,' said Henry. 'All very mysterious. Could never establish where it was all being done.'

'I could hazard a guess,' said Pawley.

'I'm sure you could,' said Dr Bee.

'What makes you think Hill's going?' Henry asked.

'He was looking around for work in England when he was on leave last year,' said Dr Bee.

'So he was,' said Pawley. 'But he said the only jobs going were for security guards.'

'Your but may be misplaced,' said Dr Bee.

Hill had been in the military though no one quite knew where or in what.

'National service finished years ago,' said Henry. 'He's far too young for that.'

'Vietnam,' said Pawley.

'Still too young.'

'Malvinas.'

'Too old.'

'SAS,' said Pawley.

'Foreign legion,' said Dr Bee.

Hill kept his hair close-cropped, and had that smiling, simmering aggression of ex-commandoes and people who had done time. He hadn't been seen in the common room for years. But fewer and fewer people had. He stopped going to the faculty club after a spot check had flushed him out as never having paid his dues.

Once a month or so he would be seen in his room, door open to demonstrate he was not engaged in sexual intercourse with a student, bookshelves totally devoid of books to demonstrate he was not engaged in anything. Once smoking was banned in university buildings he stopped coming in altogether, except possibly to take his classes. He took his name off his door. Two screw holes and a less faded patch indicated where it had been.

'Bailiffs after you?' asked Dr Bee.

'A secret admirer must have souvenired it,' he said, but he put in no requisition to have it replaced.

'Hardly worth it now,' he said to Dr Bee at target practice. They were in the same pistol club.

'That gun's unreliable,' Dr Bee told him.

'All I can afford,' he said. 'Have to rob a bank before I get a better one.'

Then he took to breeding Rottweilers.

It was not long before the bank was robbed. There was a sudden eruption of sirens into the still of the common room one afternoon.

'I hate the way,' said Gervaise, 'that students hire trucks and go around the grounds standing in the back of them with loud hailers advertising some dance or rock and roll concert.'

'Go down and tell them,' said Dr Bee.

Gervaise walked across to peer out of the window. 'Whole lot of ground staff cordoning off the road,' he said.

There was another wail of sirens.

'Couple of car loads of police now,' he reported. 'Reminds me of that old Oxford story of a gang of labourers digging up the road, did you ever hear it?'

'Certainly did,' said Dr Bee and Pawley, waving their farewells.

He told it to the empty room regardless. 'Good yarn. Bears repeating. Students went along and told the police there was a gang of students dressed as labourers digging up the Broad. Then they told the labourers a gang of students dressed as police were coming to arrest them. Jolly fracas.' He chuckled to himself in the empty room. More and more, for all of them, it was a matter of chuckling to yourself.

The police activity turned out to be real. The campus bank had been held up.

'If anything is real,' said Pawley. 'Probably an inside job.'

'Very probably,' said Dr Bee.

The security cameras had recorded the episode. A balaclava helmeted gunman. And then nothing. Vanished.

'Must have known his way around,' said Henry.

'Almost certainly,' agreed Dr Bee.

A week later the bank was hit again.

'Very professional,' said Henry. 'Very cool to come back so soon.'

'Or very unprofessional,' said Dr Bee. 'Some local Raffles, amateur cracksman.'

Gervaise got up and left.

But it had been a splendid occasion. Edwina and the Head of Department had been in the queue and the balaclava helmeted gunman had made everyone lie down on the floor.

'Down, wantons, down,' he had ordered them. 'Grovel.'

'What I'd give for a copy of the security video of that,' said Dr Bee. 'Edwina and the Head of Department prone on the floor. A gun at their heads.'

'Really?' said Pawley. 'There was really a gun at their heads? Why wasn't it fired?'

'It jammed,' said Dr Bee in disgust.

Mid-semester break came and went. Now it was downhill all the way. As usual after the break most students just stopped coming to class. The end was in sight and they were all too busy at their full-time part-time jobs to turn up any more. Hill stopped turning up too. It took two or three weeks before anyone noticed. If left to the students to notice it might never have been known at all. But the registrar phoned up the Head of Department saying they'd received Hill's letter of resignation and where was the rest of the paperwork? Hill was demanding his pension.

In the common room reactions were divided along gender lines. From the males there was nothing but envy.

'If the damn wife and the lawyers hadn't taken me to the cleaners I'd join him,' said Gervaise.

'I thought you'd already taken the retirement package,' said Dr Bee.

'So I have,' said Gervaise. 'Funny how you forget these things.'

Henry phone up the superannuation board to find out the earliest he could go and what the pension would be.

Pawley dreamed of Morocco and Thailand and Mexico, transported on the drug of travel, detached from the pain around.

The Head of Department and the girls were ecstatic. Another man down.

Henry was in the department late one evening faxing his Japanese translator. He found Dr Bee in the office.

'What, no domestic duties?' asked Henry.

'Between shifts,' said Dr Bee.

They walked down the oppressive corridors together.

'Let me show you something,' said Dr Bee.

He took out his keys and opened the blank door of Hill's room.

'How d'you manage that?' asked Henry.

'He gave me his key,' said Dr Bee. '"I shan't be coming back so I won't be needing this," were his words.'

The room was totally bare, desolate, no books, nothing on the desk, not even a Pirelli poster behind the door. So had it always been.

Dr Bee gestured to a standard issue tall metal cupboard.

'I've never know what these are for,' said Henry. 'Gowns, who wears a gown anyway?'

Dr Bee opened it.

A woollen balaclava lay on the single shelf.

20

Literary Lunch

Henry stood groaning in front of the pigeonholes, holding out a letter in one hand in passable imitation of Hamlet.

'Good news from your agent?' asked Dr Bee.

'Agent, what agent?' said Henry. 'My agent is a secret agent. She doesn't reveal her existence to me, or mine to any publisher. No, there's this letter saying Rowley said to get in touch with me and thanking me for arranging lunch and I can't read the signature. Can't remember arranging any lunch.'

'Must have arranged it after lunch,' said Dr Bee. He took the proferred letter.

'"Lunch and/or reading" it says.'

'Is that what that bit's about. Reading? What's he going to read?'

'You're sure it's a he?'

'I'm not sure of anything. Can you make out the signature?'

'Academic hand,' said Dr Bee. 'Designed so no one can decipher your notes when looking over your shoulder in the British Library.' He studied it. 'Completely impenetrable. There was an old antiquarian in the town I grew up in. Spent a quarter of a century transcribing the sixteenth and seventeenth century court records. Trouble was when he'd finished no one could read the transcriptions. Not even himself. Still not published. True story,' he added.

'I have no doubt,' said Henry.

'I give it you for when inspiration fails.'

'Inspiration has never failed me,' Henry snapped. Rashly, perhaps. He was usually cautious not to tempt the muses. But he was frustrated by the letter, annoyed at the indecipherability of its signature, alarmed at his lack of memory of arranging whatever seemed to have been arranged.

Rowley bailed him up in the corridor.

'You'll fix up that welcoming lunch for Francesca,' he said, in the form of a question, but a demand, always a demand.

'Francesca?' said Henry, a question, almost a plea. 'Welcoming?'

'Francesca Templar,' said Rowley. 'The novelist. I told her to write to you.'

'Ah.'

'Invite a few kindred spirits across to the faculty club, put it on the account.'

'Your account?' said Henry.

'Not my account,' said Rowley, 'the departmental account.'

'Ah,' said Henry.

'May not be able to get there myself,' said Rowley. 'Function over at the American Center. So play mother, Henry, would you mind?'

Henry put round a circular. Please let me know if you are interested in having a welcoming lunch with novelist Francesca Templar who will be visiting the department as writer-in-residence. No one replied. They never did reply. Their individual, internalized sense of inadequacy at meeting anyone distinguished, however minimally so, together with their collective resentment at meeting anyone succesful, however notionally, ensured they would never come to lunch. Why would they come to lunch to meet a writer? This was a department of English Literature and Cultural Studies. They had no time for writers. They had an ingrained hostility to the creative. They loathed living literature. Henry tried the direct method but the Head of Department had a promotions committee meeting that day which would stretch into lunch, Gervaise had to see a chap about a boat, Phillipa didn't think so, not indigenous enough, Dr Bee and Pawley refused point blank.

'Not lunch,' said Dr Bee. 'Not the sacred hour.'

'Can't smoke in the faculty club,' said Pawley. 'Wouldn't survive it without a smoke.'

Henry called up his poet friend Sam Samson. 'She's famous,' he said. 'Powerful. Get you published internationally.'

'Will I have to fuck her?' Sam asked.

'Just give her a book,' said Henry.

And then Brett Happenstanz expressed a wish to meet her. So he invited him along as well.

Brett Happenstanz was Henry's new drinking friend. Pawley was useless in the evenings, sat in front of the television with a bag of dope and refused to venture out.

'Feral dogs,' he insisted. 'Feral dogs and federal agents. Safest to stay at home. Might get abducted by aliens.'

'Abducted at home or on the streets?' asked Henry.

'Who knows?' said Pawley.

And Dr Bee was too busy commuting between his wife and his mistress and his girl friend. He was sometimes good for a quick aperitif in the club at five, but as soon as the rush hour parking restrictions lifted he had to rendezvous in a restaurant.

So Brett Happenstanz had been a gift from the gods, a bolt from the blue. Someone to have a drink with after the day's writing was done, and the day's writing was done on the Thomas Mann principle, within two hours. Happenstanz was out of town for the summer. No one stayed in town for the summer, no one who was anyone. And Happenstanz was surely someone, with his London apartment and his visiting writers' programme at the University of Surleighwick. Bragg, Bellow, Singer, Grass. The names fell like raindrops in an Apollinaire poem. So when you pass through next time, Henry. . . . It hung there, a stage in a grand itinerary, something to take up once the other details were in place, a standing invitation.

Brett liked to hang out in the Texas saloon, a bar adorned with saddles and whips and cow-horns and frequented by young cowpokes in jeans and boots and leather and studs. Happenstanz and Henry would sit there demolishing white wine by the bottle, planning an international review of literature and all the arts.

'I know this woman,' Happenstanz had said. He peered across at some fresh faced young dude with a red bandana furled fetchingly round its throat.

'Stinking rich. Used to be Castro's mistress. Amazing person. Lives in the South of France. Comes across to London to buy modern first editions. Now she wants to be involved in something creative like this. How much do you reckon it would need?'

'You can run it at a loss for five years,' said Henry, 'so there are tax minimisation advantages.'

'She'd know all about that,' said Happenstanz. 'Who should we put in it?'

'He's intelligence,' said Pawley.

'Not much sign of it,' said Dr Bee.

'He just wants to know who all your contacts are,' said Pawley.

'You think?' said Henry. 'Could be, I suppose. Still, if they funded *Encounter* and *Partisan* and *Quadrant,* why shouldn't they fund me?'

'Do you want an answer to that?' asked Dr Bee, 'or would you prefer to let the mind roam free?'

'I think an international review of art and literature would be a nice idea,' said Henry. 'Properly funded, of course. Properly funded I could take a couple of years' leave to get it established. It could be my way out of here.'

'It could indeed,' said Dr Bee. '*The Alcatraz Chronicle. The Attica Annual. The Pentonville Papers, The San Quentin Quarterly. The Long Bay Review of Books.*'

Sam Samson phoned to say he was going to be late, he was in town, he was going to be on television. Henry said meet us in the faculty club, which was what he had told Francesca' publisher's publicist to tell Francesca. Happenstanz was already there with a bottle of Hunter Valley semillon he'd ordered on Henry's account.

'I don't have an account, put it on the department's account,' he told the barman.

'No problems, Henry,' said the barman.

And then Francesca Templar arrived, all fluffed out hair and scarlet lips and presence, she had presence. Happenstanz poured her a glass of wine but she asked for mineral water. 'Peanuts, too. While we wait,' he ordered, and began investigating their mutual acquaintance in London. Germs. Clive. Kylie.

In due and belated course Sam stumbled in with his latest inseparable wife. They both had the yellow tinge of imminent liver failure.

'It was hell,' he said. 'They filmed it at crack of dawn. Before dawn. I got up at four.'

'You didn't go to bed,' said Sara.

'That's right, I didn't go to bed,' said Sam.

'This is Francesca Templar,' said Henry.

'I've got your book,' said Sam.

'There are several,' said Francesca.

'Volumes,' said Happenstanz. 'Shelves. Warehouses,' he added expansively.

'I've got them all,' said Sam, 'but this is the one.'

He delved into his woven Greek bag and produced a copy of his own *Selected Poems.*

'This is for you,' he said. 'I brought it specially.'

He passed it across to her and dug deeper into the bag. His latest volume. Three bottles of pills. His scrap book. And then the book of Templar. It still had the REDUCED sticker on it. Originally $39.95, now $2.95.

'I'll get you to sign it.'

He passed it across and grabbed back his own, sending Happenstanz's glass pouring its contents over the book of Templar.

'Oh shit,' said Sam, standing up, delving into his pockets for a handkerchief to mop up the wine. He found one. It was disgusting. Happenstanz shuddered and clicked his fingers for the barman to bring a cloth over.

'Don't worry, I'll wipe it off,' said Sam, smeering wine and snot over the table's surface before reaching across for his *Selected* and opening it at the title page to sign it.

'It seems to be signed already,' said Francesca.

'They come like that,' said Henry.

'Oh shit,' said Sam, 'so it is. I meant to give this to that TV interviewer. I must have given him the wrong one.'

He crossed out the inscription and began to write Francesca's name above it. The spelling proved too hard so he stopped after F.

'That interview,' he said. 'It was a nightmare. It's an arts programme so they only get to use the studio when no one else wants it. I had to take all these pills to stay awake.'

It reminded him to take more and he delved into his Greek bag again and produced a bottle. He emptied a couple of pills into his hand and tossed them into his mouth. They stuck in his throat and he reached out for something with which to swill them down. Happenstanz's glass was empty and he was preoccupied in mopping its contents from Francesca Templar's thighs. Sam took a swig from Francesca's mineral water.

She shuddered, whether in delight at Happenstanz's ministrations or in distaste at Sam she did not say.

'You might as well have the rest,' said Francesca.

'Sure?' said Sam.

'Quite sure.'

Sam took another swig.

'Do you want one of these?' he said, reciprocating Francesca's gesture, offering her the bottle of pills.

'What are they?' asked Happenstanz.

'Some sort of opium,' said Sam. 'They're for cancer patients. And alcoholics. They give them to alcoholics to stop them drinking. Here, try some.'

'The last thing I want to do is to stop drinking,' said Happenstanz.

'You can still drink with them,' said Sam. 'They're great. They're the only thing that got me through the interview. That man's a space animal.'

'He was totally pilled up,' said Sara, surfacing from the labours of reapplying her make-up, mascara, lipstick, and nose and eye-drops. 'Every time he asked a question and the camera moved to Samuel he'd pop another pill. He couldn't read the idiot board. He couldn't remember the beginning of a sentence by the time he got to the end.'

'I offered to swap him a bottle of mine for a bottle of his,' said Sam, 'but he pretended not to hear.'

'He couldn't hear, he was out of it,' said Sara.

'He said was I like Rimbaud?' said Sam. 'I said "Yes." "In what way?" he said. "Any way," I said. Then he couldn't think of anything else to say. He kept asking me how long I was in gaol and I kept saying I don't want to talk about gaol, life's a gaol, television's a gaol, after this I'm going to the university and that's a gaol. "That's very interesting," he said. "No, it's not," I said, "Have you ever been in gaol? It's totally uninteresting."'

'That's when he lost it altogether,' said Sara. 'I think he probably had been in gaol. He was probably out on day release or something.'

'Is anybody hungry?' asked Francesca.

'Not really,' said Sam. 'You don't feel like eating on these tablets. Here, try one.' He brought out his pills again.

'Bit early yet, isn't it?' said Happenstanz. He held up an empty semillon bottle to the barman. 'Another of these,' he said.

'We can get a drink in the dining room,' said Henry taking pity on Francesca.

'Oh, in that case,' said Happenstanz, 'let's go in there when we've finished this one.'

He filled his and Henry's glass from the new bottle.

Francesca fixed her eyes on it, calculating how long it would be before they drank it.

'Not long at all,' said Happenstanz. 'Soon demolish that.'

They got to the dining room just as it had shut.

'We're not too late, are we?' asked Henry.

'I'll see,' said the ear-ringed ex-con who ladled out the soup.

The cook's boy friend, Basil, the relief barman, emerged. He had his sleeves rolled up and slivers of ice were spread through his hair and eyebrows.

'Been breaking up frozen beef for meat pies,' he said. 'Got it on special. Best of British.'

'Meet Francesca Templar,' said Henry. 'The writer.'

'Honoured, I'm sure,' said Basil. 'What can I do for you?'

'Could we eat?' said Henry.

'I have to eat,' said Francesca.

'Eat?' said Basil. 'Ah well, let me see, let me see Henry, why don't you take a table and I'll see what we have left. The beef needs to thaw out a bit.'

'Drinks?' said Happenstanz.

'Good idea,' said Basil, 'have a drink while I see what we can rustle up.'

'Man after my own heart,' said Happenstanz. 'A rustler.'

They settled down at a table. Happenstanz brought over a couple of bottles of wine.

'This is all on the department, isn't it?' he asked Henry. 'No point in getting cheap stuff if the department's paying.'

Basil came and stood at their table.

'Let me tell you the story of my life while the chef cooks something up,' he said. He smiled winningly at Francesca. 'As a writer you might find it interesting. It would make a fascinating book.'

'Could we order first?' asked Francesca.

'No point,' said Basil, 'no need, they'll just send up what they have.'

He drew up a chair and poured himself a glass of wine.

'I used to be a geographer,' he began, 'but my true love was music.'

'Music?' said Sam. 'Why not poetry?'

'Poetry, too,' said Basil.

'Good,' said Sam.

'Fiction?' asked Happenstanz. 'After all, we have novelists present.' He beamed graciously at Francesca and Henry, letting them know he had their interests at heart.

'Oh yes, and fiction,' said Basil.

'Excellent,' said Happenstanz.

'But to make a living I was a geographer. And then I went

mad.'

Sara reached her hand across to him and laid it on his arm. 'Oh, a real madman.'

'I had a breakdown. My wife left me. She took my house. I took study leave, long service leave, sick leave, leave of my senses. Geography offered no consolations. I took a job as a barman. I fell in love with the cook. Happiness came back into my life. I took up music again. Couldn't you make a novel out of that?' he asked Francesca.

He vanished.

'Is he going to serve us?' asked Francesca.

'When you show him your novel,' said Happenstanz. 'When he is satisfied with the way you have portrayed him.'

'I took up the violin,' said Basil, re-entering, bearing it with him. 'I would like to play you a tune. A little piece of Bach. And then one of my own compositions. You will have to bear with me a little. The stress of my breakdown meant I lost control of my bowing arm. Sometimes it goes spastic.'

'Like Sam,' said Sara.

'I cannot control it. But amongst friends I know you'll undcrtand.'

He played for them in the deserted club. It was like the depths of wildest Hungary in midwinter, the gypsies in from the plains, Francesca encamped alongside, gathering material for her next book. Sara danced for them amongst the tables, Happenstanz rose and joined her, a model of courtesy and old world charm. Sam analysed one of his poems for Francesca, flicking through the pages, comparing thematic treatments over the course of his career.

'Sure you won't have a tablet?' he offered. 'They take away your hunger. You don't need to eat with these. That's why I'm not worried about no food coming. They're great like that.'

He emptied some out onto the table and held a couple between his thumb and forefinger, reaching across to Francesca's pursed lips.

'Would you like a copy of my poems?' said Sam.

'That might be nice,' said Francesca.

'Signed or unsigned.'

'Oh, signed,' said Francesca.

'Then I'd have to fuck you,' said Sam.

Sara took a swipe at him and fell over and twisted her ankle.

'Ice,' said Henry, 'that's what you need. Stops the swelling. Get some ice from the bar.'

'All right,' said Basil, 'if you insist.' Still bowing away.

'I do,' said Henry.

'Help yourself to ice,' he said. 'But I have something better.'

Happenstanz went off to the bar for the ice and brought another bottle of white to be going on with. He ministered to Sara with one hand full of ice and to himself with a full glass, chilling it with one of the ice cubes from Sara's feet.

'Your tiny ankle is frozen,' he sang.

'A gentleman,' she said. 'After all these fucking years.'

Basil returned with his didgeridoo.

'Healing music,' he said.

He pointed it at Sara's ankle and began to blow, the deep reverberating tones throbbing around the ankle and around Brett Happenstanz and around Sam, declaiming his poems, and around Henry and around Francesca Templar herself, head in hands.

21

Imagining the Gym

'This place,' said Henry. 'It's impossible. It's beyond the human imagination. How can I ever write fiction when this passes for reality?'

'Could you ever?' asked Dr Bee. 'I thought that was why you took a day job, so you could be a writer without having to write for a living.'

'I imagine,' said Pawley, more generously, 'your problem is that you find the material so distasteful you can't bear to write about it.'

That was it. Precisely. 'Couldn't have put it better myself,' said Henry.

'That's positive praise indeed,' said Dr Bee.

But it was true. How could he bear to immerse himself in it, the felt life, the daily lived experience? He devoted his major efforts to keeping himself clear of it, fending off the awful tactility of the pervasive horror, directing his thoughts to anything else rather than dwell on it even momentarily. It was like there was an ectoplasm possessing the university, sucking everyone and everything into its mortal embrace, pouring its digestive juices over them all and feeding on them alive as they stuck there, trapped. You could hear its pulsations, a dull hum of decay through the building as the research assistants assembled research for the Dead Hand, for the Head of Department, for Philippa, for Gervaise, for Rowley.

How could he bear to contemplate it, how could he bear to have it lodge in his consciousness? Even to consider it put the observer at risk. But to enter it, to probe, to dissect, to record, to clone, to replicate was to surely to run the danger of terminal infection, like a neuro-surgeon opening up a brain diseased with kuru.

The women's gym, for instance. What did he know about it? He knew they met, Philippa and the Head of Department and Edwina and more, regular trysts among the whatever. Among the what? He could not even visualise it, preferred not to attempt to, ropes or parallel bars or treadmills or nautiluses. Were they nautiluses or nautili? He had no idea and preferred to keep it that way. He ran the spellcheck. It accepted both versions and then told him gratuitously, that Pawley was not in the dictionary. It instructed change to Poley, with additional suggestions of Palely or Parley.

Gym had been a horror for him at school. The thought of voluntarily exploring another gym, the thought of imagining Edwina and the Head of Department and Philippa doing unspeakable things, working out, sweating, showering together, distaste was too mild a word. Repugnance. And yet he knew they all met there on the torture machines, locked into their S and M delights, getting fitter and fitter the better to torment him and Dr Bee and Pawley, Poley, Palely, Parley and Gervaise. He couldn't say he minded about Gervaise. If anyone deserved torture and torment, Gervaise was it. But they wouldn't stay satisfied with that. If they found they did a good job with Gervaise they would extend their range.

Duty required him to penetrate the sanctum. What sort of novelist was he if he was afraid of peering through the shower curtains? A writer of taste, discretion and decorum and who was going to care about that? Maybe he could bribe the management for inside information. It wasn't royalty he would be snooping on, surely it wouldn't cost that much, his research funds could cover it.

Or why not use the imagination? The novelist's tool. Why be restricted to fact and data? Why be entrapped by truth and representation? Why not free himself and win the Booker, be a magic realist, a post-modernist, a creature of the way we live now? Couldn't he imagine them swinging on the ropes and plotting how to give Dr Bee ten first year tutorials? There they were leaping over the wooden horse they called Gervaise, exchanging ideas on how to block Pawley's leave application. Up and up they bounced on the trampoline, tossing up idea upon idea of how to purge the department of thc masculine. Was it so unimaginable? Surely he thought of it every day, despite himself. He suspected he dreamed of it every night, those nightmares that woke him in terror and whose detail he was so grateful not to be able to recall, he knew in his heart of hearts what they were about, they were about this, the Head of Department and Philippa and Edwina and their ilk, whacking into the punchballs, punchballs with lip-sticked, mascara'd faces representing him and his like, the male, the male being punched and pummelled and pulped into oblivion by the sisterhood. He knew all too well what was going on, it just needed fleshing out, imaginative empathy, it just needed the detail filling in with everything that he found himself recoiling from.

'No,' said Pawley, 'That's all old stuff. You've read too much Buchan and Hemingway. This is the modern world. It's all steroids and amphetamines now, that's what gyms are all about. All the press-ups and push-ups are just a front, it's a dealers' paradise. They don't grow muscles like that from punching punchballs. They grow them from taking steroids. It's like commercial beef production. Feed 'em chemicals. You've seen Philippa's forearms.'

He broke into a spontaneous sweat of remembrance even as he spoke. Seen them, he'd even felt them, he'd had them wrapped around him like Laocoon enmeshed by the serpent. The Lamia of literary theory built up on the steroids of post-structuralism.

'All that lycra and aerobics, that's just the respectable face of addiction. Where do you think they get all their energy from? Not from working out, let alone making out. It's the chemical life, as Auden put it. How do they have the staying power for all those committees? Because they're bombed. They just sit there in a spaced out trance. They're like third world working women in the paddy fields, chewing betel nut, keeps them going, keeps them narcotised. You think those slavering red lips and blood red teeth of the Head of Department and Edwina and Philippa are the mark of the vampire? Too Gothic, Henry, those days are gone. Just because they teach *Frankenstein* on fifteen separate courses doesn't mean they spend the rest of the time reading *Dracula*. No, it's the red stain of the betel nut. They're heavy substance abusers.

'Why do you think the Head of Department is so loghorrheic? Why can she never shut up? You've heard her at staff meetings. Yes, yes, yes. She's like Sartre after his daily benzedrine and whisky, the endless refusal of closure. Why else the piercing glassy eyes? Why else the inability to hear anything anyone else says?'

In Pawley's vision of the gym the ropes were neatly furled

against the wall bars, the wooden horse was safely stabled in the store room. The punch balls designated Henry, Gervaise, Dr Bee and himself may well have been ranked along the wall, but they were not reeling from blows. No, the girls stood passively in line as their daily dose of steroids and amphetamines was doled out, swilled down with an orange juice looking suspiciously like methadone, followed by a chaser of mixed vitamins. And then they were off. Rave, rave, rave.

'I admire their stamina,' said Pawley. 'I've tried that stuff. It's all lethal. They live in a perpetual haze of anti-inflammatories and amphetamine-based diet pills and valium and serapax and prozac and steroids. They're untouchable. They're like berserkers. They're full-on junkies. You can't tangle with them. Just leave them alone at the gym and pray for kidney failure. It won't be long.'

Dr Bee had a different vision again. It was not that he rejected Henry's reading of sadistic violence, nor dismissed Pawley's informed account of substance abuse. He found both appealing but added his own further possibilities.

He speculated first on pistol practice, the girls lying there in swim suits and ear-muffs, sighting down the barrel at cut-out targets, the usual subjects. Then they moved to bayoneting, rushing out at stuffed dummies and gouging away at the straw or foam rubber or whatever dummies were stuffed with now. After that it was unarmed combat and his smile softened as he saw them hurling each other round the gym, wearing those elegant martial arts uniforms that provocatively fell open for the salacious imagination, pinning each other down on the mats and panting into each others' ears, sitting astride each other in indubitably erotic body contact, frozen in still-life poses of exquisite, violent sensuality. It was not far from this to a vision of combat in the field, practical mud wrestling, he loved it, their faces smeared and streaked with camouflage like the big cats, prowling predatory mammals in wet t-shirts, pressing each other into therapeutic mud baths, it was a vision of Pompeii before the lava hardened.

His throat throbbed and pulsed like Toad of Toad Hall, a reverie of nursery idylls, exquisitely literary, the undifferentiated sexuality of breasts and buttocks and sisterly brutality.

'Why don't we branch out for lunch?' he suggested. 'What about that pub that offers lingerie waitresses, live shows and jelly wrestling? Bring your own spoon, it says.' He produced one from his pocket, bent already from the force of the imagination.

22

Writer-in-Residence

It was Rowley who had arranged the writer-in-residence. The one thing you could say for the Dead Hand and the Head of Department was they would never invite any visitor. For them there was no outside world. All was the solipsistic negation of the deus absconditus. But Rowley was of the Have Degree, Will Travel professorial mode. International co-operation. I'll do something for the USA and then the USA will find something for me to do for it.

'You'd have thought I might have been consulted,' said Henry.

'Not really,' said Pawley.

'Or at least informed.'

'Not at all.'

'As a novelist myself, does my expertise count for nothing?' asked Henry.

'Absolutely.'

'Just as a matter of common courtesy,' said Henry. 'Human decency.'

Pawley laughed.

Other than Henry's pique there was no reaction. The department greeted the arrival of Francesca Templar as it greeted most other things, with that dull indifference usually ascribed to indigenous peoples suffering the depradations of colonial rule. Nothing enlivened the listless eye, the enervated shuffle. The doors remained as closed to casual visitors as those of any desert township, the corridors as silent and menacing as the alleys of any plague stricken medieval village.

But Francesca Templar, who had been writer-in-residence at more institutions than any of you all have had hot dinners, as she genially announced at morning tea, was blandly indifferent to the vast indifference. The world was but a sounding box for her theatre of one. She welcomed silent adulation and interpreted all silence as adulation. She had that characteristic megalomania of the internationally acclaimed writer. She was unstoppable.

And she presented herself well. Groomed. Polished. Dr Bee eyed her appraisingly. He was prepared to be polite. It was always a worrying politeness, as if designed to extract confidences that could be later impaled. It had an over-enunciated quality, signifying politeness too markedly. But Francesca, nothing if not over-enunciated herself, received it with the Olympian detachment she received everything, paring her finger nails and buffing them with the free manicure set distributed to business-class airline passengers.

'I asked her,' said Dr Bee, 'what she thought of Tuscan Bayes. That insufferable creature Henry brought in for a reading years ago.'

'"What did I think of him?" she said. "It's in my *Memoirs of the*

Sacred Rage, Chapter two. About page thirty-seven, I think you'll find. I capture him there. Rather well, according to the *London Review of Books*. And one can't say better than that, can one?"'

'Self-promotion. Marketing. Hype,' said Henry with a weary admiration. 'How are they able to do it, day in, day out? Did she offer to sell you a copy?'

'Insufferable little carpetbagger,' said Dr Bee. 'She started to open that great travel bag she carries. That's no doubt what she was doing. I left. Drank the rest of my tea over the sink.'

'Spilled some on your waistcoat,' said Henry.

'Did she tell you she was mugged?' said Pawley.

'Pinned against a wall,' said Henry.

'By a big bold black man panting with desire,' said Pawley.

'He who steals her purse steals trash,' said Dr Bee. 'The story stopped just as it was getting interesting.'

'She told me about the trauma of it,' said Henry. 'Wept copiously on my shoulder. Had to get the jacket dry-cleaned.'

'She told me she still has nightmares about it,' said Pawley. 'Phoned me up at three in the morning. She'd just had one.'

'Very graphic about the black chap's breathing,' said Henry. 'Could feel the hot gusts and the throbbing pulse as she was telling me. I wonder if she writes like that. Ought to have a look at her stuff one day, maybe.'

'But then she cuts out,' said Dr Bee. 'It's all the old bodice ripping stuff. I want to know, did she do it?'

'Do what?' asked Henry.

'Go down on the mugger,' said Dr Bee. 'Or did he escape?'

'Did *he* escape? Surely she was the one being attacked,' said Henry.

'You've met her, Henry,' said Dr Bee. 'Who do you think was the aggressor in an encounter like that? In a dark alley. In the bowels of Gommorah.'

'Well, I don't know about that.'

'You take the story too simply, Henry,' said Dr Bee. 'Where is your suspicion? Where is your critical training? The pleasures of the sub-text. Never underestimate the predatory instinct. All those midnight phone calls. Floods of tears. Sleepless nights. I think they're all for the one that got away.'

'What I can't stand,' said Dr Bee, 'is the way she sits in the common room all day with the door open, waiting for the phone to ring in her own room.'

'Hollywood calling,' said Pawley. 'Or Langley, Virginia.'

'Every time it rings she scuttles in there like a rabbit on heat. Why doesn't she just wait in her own room?'

'That way no one would know she was constantly on call. She needs us to know how often she's called,' said Pawley. 'Her publisher, her agent, her publicist. How do you manage, Henry? You got an answering service or something?'

'Did I tell you the joke about the agent calling?' said Henry.

'Yes,' said Pawley.

'Many times,' said Dr Bee.

'Chap gets home and his wife tells him the car's been wrecked, the house burned down -'

'And oh, yes, your agent called. Really? My agent? What a marvellous day,' said Dr Bee and Pawley in concert.

'You've heard it?' said Henry.

'You should tell it to Francesca Templar.'

'I did,' said Henry, 'that's what reminded me.'

'Had she heard it?'

'Don't know,' said Henry. 'Claimed she couldn't understand it, anyway. "But my agent's always calling," she said.'

'Don't we know,' said Dr Bee. 'Can't drink a cup of tea in peace without her leaping up and pushing past.'

In the end Dr Bee took to phoning Francesca on the common room phone and watching her drop her *New York Review of Books,* stumble through the chairs and rush to her room to pick up the phone. Then Dr Bee would hang up.

'Poor little blighter. She'd been waiting there twenty-five minutes and no one had rung. Felt I had to put her out of her misery.'

He was still standing by the phone one morning when she came back in.

'Who were you calling?' she demanded.

'I shouldn't have thought it was any business of yours,' said Dr Bee.

'Yes it is,' Francesca said. 'You were calling me.'

'Two questions,' said Dr Bee. 'Why ask if you know? And why would I call you when I can speak to you across the table?'

'You called me from there and hung up.'

'Why would I do that?' asked Dr Bee. 'Never mind, I'm sure they'll call again if it was important.'

He went back to his room and dialled her again. Just to have the last silence.

Henry put on a reading for her. He asked the administrative assistant to book a room, scribbled out a note announcing it for the administrative assistant to type and put in everyone's pigeonhole, and retreated exhausted to lunch.

'Very chivalrous of you,' said Pawley.

'She asked me to,' said Henry.

'That was polite of her.'

'Well, insisted,' conceded Henry. 'She said "When I am invited to a university a public reading is always arranged."

'Really,' Henry had said.

'But I see no sign of one here,' she said.

'Better ask the Head of Department,' Henry said.

'I already have,' she said, 'and she said that this was your area.'

'My area.'

'She said you always organised visiting readings.'

'Did she? I organised one once. It was some time ago. No one came. Students just aren't interested any more. In the past, with end of year examinations on the whole year's work, they used to come to see if they could pick up something useful. But now it's all semesterised and modularised. They do their course, write their assignment, sell off the books. There's no sense of a general literary education any more. They won't come to anything not part of an examinable course.'

'I'm not interested in your pedagogic problems,' she said. 'I expect a reading.'

'Right,' said Henry.

'And I expect books on sale.'

'Books on sale?' said Henry. 'People don't usually buy books these days. We tend to wait till titles are remaindered and then give copies away.'

'Isn't there a campus bookstore?'

'Well, yes,' said Henry. 'For text books. Not for -' He was going to say literature but baulked. Could he call Francesca's books literature? 'Not for modern fiction,' he said.

'Then get onto my publishers,' she said. 'Get them to arrange something with the bookstore.'

She smiled graciously at him.

'I'm willing to sign copies,' she said. 'I don't mind doing that. On occasions like this.'

Henry poured the wine with a shaking hand. A pale white from the Abruzzi. Though not as pale as Francesca had turned him.

'I phoned her publisher,' he said. 'They're my publisher too. It's all too terrible.'

Pawley pushed the plate of antipasto across.

'Here, eat something before you keel over.'

Henry absently complied.

'I phoned up. Gave my name. "Who?" they said. "One of your authors," I said. "Oh, an author," they said. With that doubt and contempt publishers and media people and arts administrators and university senior management get into their voice. Even Foreign Affairs are either simply hostile or paranoid. But this contempt -'

'Why couldn't she phone her publisher herself?' Dr Bee asked.

'She had to in the end,' said Henry. 'They put me on hold and no one came. I sat there listening to some vile jingle. Then the line went dead. "I tried," I told her. Better to have tried and failed than never to have tried at all.

'"Try harder," she said.

'That was it. "Can't do," I said. "Have to dash. Business appointment. Got to see my accountant. You'd better call them. Let me know how you get on."'

'And when was all this?' asked Dr Bee.

'Ten minutes ago,' said Henry. 'Thank the Lord we had lunch arranged. Otherwise I'd have slit my wrists.' He sucked up the wine. 'Or hers,' he said, revivifying, the frozen blood coursing back into his veins.

'Mug her,' said Dr Bee. 'Then she'd love you for life.'

The day of the reading Henry insisted on an early lunch across the road at the pub.

'Twelve-thirty,' said Dr Bee.

'Twelve at the latest,' said Henry. 'More like 11.45. 11.30 even. Brunch.'

'Brunch,' said Dr Bee with distaste. 'Is this the influence of our visiting writer? A new familiarity with degraded terms?'

'Probably,' Henry conceded. He was ready to concede anything. 'I have to introduce her confounded reading at one. Can't sit all through that without a bite to eat.

'And a drop to drink.'

'Absolutely.'

'I'd have thought you would have been entertaining her,' said Dr Bee. 'Wining and dining and exuding international charm.'

'She never eats before readings,' said Henry. 'Finds it interferes with the flow.'

'Sounds horribly gynaecological,' said Dr Bee.

Henry shuddered. 'She explained it all to me,' he said. 'It is like the divine furor. The Sibyl. *Aeneid* book six. I think she even told me the line numbers. She has to be ready for the God to enter her.'

'And are you poised for this penetration?' asked Dr Bee.

'I find her increasingly distasteful by the minute,' said Henry. 'I tried to tell her it wouldn't be a big occasion. We don't have big occasions any more. I mean she'll be lucky if anybody turns up at all. No one's heard of her.'

'Did you tell her that?'

'Not exactly. I mean no one's heard of anyone any more. Not writers. Not in a Department of Literature.'

'I'd have thought you'd have put on another departmental lunch,' said Pawley.

'Just to prove the point.' said Dr Bee.

'Never again,' said Henry. 'The Head of Department is providing sandwiches at the bar afterwards.'

'What exquisite taste,' said Dr Bee.

Yes,' said Henry.

'So if it all goes wrong, as we can confidently expect, she won't be inviting you for a reciprocal reading,' said Dr Bee.

'She's already made it clear she doesn't invite people to read at her campus,' Henry said. 'One of the first things she told me.

"I wish I could," she said, "but the distinguished visitor committee organises all that. We have twenty-three Nobel prize-winners on the faculty, so we look for very distinguished visitors," she said.'

'So it doesn't matter if no one turns up,' said Pawley, 'since she's not going to ask you back.'

'Well, there won't be quite no one,' said Henry. 'You're both coming. Aren't you?'

'Up to a point,' said Dr Bee. 'We'll be with you in spirit.'

'You're not going to let me down,' said Henry. 'Are you?'

'Got it in one,' said Pawley. ''Fraid so.'

The reading had been booked into the large lecture theatre, which was a mistake. But she had insisted on it. 'It has ambience. I cannot read in a characterless box.' So she'd had her way. It made the occasion seem very empty. There was the table of her books and someone from the bookstore. Two young publishers from her multinational publisher, Fiona and Fiona. The Head of the Department. A foreign exchange student left over from an earlier mathematics class, transcribing someone's sums at the back. And Ms Chung. Henry breezed in, hair uplifted by the winnowing wind, a copy of the *Guardian Weekly* to read if it all became too insupportable.

'Did you put round notices?' asked the Head of Department.

'Certainly did,' said Henry. 'One in every pigeon hole. Usual instructions. Remind your classes. Everyone desperately welcome. Admission absolutely free.'

Francesca glowered, her rat-trap lips sinking deep into her jaw.

They stood at the lectern, the Head of Department, Fiona and Fiona, Francesca and Henry, looking at Ms Chung and the scribbling student.

The door opened and they all swung round in anticipation.

It was the ace reporter from the *University Mirror*, hot on the trail.

There was nothing to say and Henry from long experience attempted nothing.

They gave it five minutes and then another five. The Head of Department laughed nervously. 'Yes, yes, yes,' she said, 'it's a difficult time of year. Student assignments. Meetings. Pressures.'

'I have never, in all my career,' said Francesca, 'experienced this.'

'Really?' said Henry. 'Ah well, at least we can offer something new. A first for us.'

'Perhaps we should go across to the faculty club,' said the Head of Department.

Ms Chung bought a book and brought it across to Francesca. She slipped a polaroid in to mark the spot for signing.

'Maybe you'd like to join us for a sandwich,' said Henry.

They sat in a dark corner of the club, the ace reporter from the *University Mirror* one side of her, Ms Chung the other, in rapt attention.

'And then I was mugged,' Francesca said.

'How exciting,' said Ms Chung. 'You must tell us about it. Have you written about it in many of your novels?'

The Head of Department was off caucusing at the cappuccino queue. The two Fionas stood waiting to be bought more drinks.

'So what sort of product are you looking for now?' Henry asked them, his most beaming self.

'Women's fiction,' said Fiona.

'Native peoples,' said Fiona.

'Women native peoples,' said Fiona.

'Young writers. Under thirty,' said Fiona.

'We've cleared out all that old dead white male list,' said Fiona.

'Pulped it all,' said Fiona.

'With great satisfaction,' said Fiona.

'And utter finality,' said Fiona.

'All turned into egg cartons,' said Fiona.

'Back in a moment,' said Henry.

He stood at the urinal, away from it all, and made his decision.

'I could see there was no place for me any more,' he said. 'So I just walked off.'

'Wise decision,' said Dr Bee.

'No place ever? Or just no place this afternoon?' asked Pawley.

'I thought you'd both still be here.'

'Just because we start lunch early doesn't mean we have to finish early,' said Dr Bee.

'I might order another carafe then,' said Henry. He waved across at the waiter. 'No sense in going back this afternoon. Wait till it all blows over.'

'You could be here for a few years,' said Dr Bee.

23

Administrative Matters

The Head of Department sent round a circular announcing that she was willing and able to continue on as Head of Department for another year.

'What about elections?' said Pawley. 'Doesn't anyone remember we have elections? Or have they been suspended? Have we entered a period of martial law?'

'Do you want to stand against her?' said Dr Bee.

'The last time I stood that fuckwit Gervaise stood as well. That's how she got in. The male vote was split, the femocracy stayed solid and triumphed.'

'She doesn't have that much support,' said Henry. 'Between the two of you you got more votes. Why didn't one of you withdraw?'

'I wasn't going to withdraw and have that reactionary clown as Head,' said Pawley. 'Anyway, I nominated first. He came in as a spoiler.'

'He'd rather have her than you,' said Henry. 'Is that it?'

'Of course that's it. For all their unreconstructed male chauvinism, the right would rather have a woman than a left-wing male. That's why they've advanced women. The reactionary good old boys like Gervaise and the Dead Hand. They're terrified of any progressive change. And they know creatures like our Head of Department are so eager for advancement they'll never change anything. Of course Gervaise would prefer her to me.'

'And you'd prefer her to him,' observed Dr Bee. 'So much for male bonding and gender solidarity.'

'I'm not convinced she won't change things,' said Henry. 'And for the worse.'

'You should stand again,' said Dr Bee like a good general, leading from behind.

'There are only so many public humiliations one can take in a lifetime,' said Pawley.

'Don't believe it,' said Dr Bee. 'There will be more.'

There was no further talk of elections. That, indeed, was the only talk of elections. The Head of Department's extended term was silently accepted. A month later another circular went round and flashed across the e-mail. The duties of Head of Department were so onerous, said the Head of Department, that it had been decided to institute a new position of Deputy Head of Department to relieve the Head of Department of the day to day housekeeping of the department.

'A housekeeper. Or maybe an au pair. That might be interesting,' said Dr Bee.

'Will she keep the $12,000 Head of Department allowance, or will they split it between them? Or will they both get an additional $12,000?' Henry asked.

'Nice work if you can get it,' said Dr Bee.

'What appals me,' said Pawley the forever appalled, 'is the

way these creatures grab the positions, take the financial perks, give themselves relief from teaching because of all the committee work, then get themselves on every faculty and university committee they can and never do the job they were so eager to get because they are so busy climbing up the ladder to the next position. Everything a stepping stone to something else. She should never have taken on the job in the first place.'

'And who would you prefer?' asked Dr Bee. 'Rowley? The Dead Hand?'

'Rowley can't do it because he's going on leave.'

'On leave?' said Dr Bee. 'How can he be going on leave? He's never even here. How can he still get leave? It's bad enough he's still on salary.'

'Everyone gets leave,' said Henry. 'The editor of the *University Mirror* is on sabbatical leave right now.'

'How can non-academic staff get study leave?' asked Dr Bee.

'Must have signed a good contract,' said Pawley. 'The package, as they call it.'

'The reason he's on leave,' said Henry, 'is they're restructuring the media office.'

'You heard this while you were down there trying to promote your latest literary offering?' said Dr Bee.

Henry smiled thinly. 'Anyway, they're restructuring and they want him out of the way. He'll be lucky if his job's there when he gets back.'

'So they give him six months off on full pay.'

'A year, actually.'

'I thought you couldn't get a year's study leave any more. I thought six months was the maximum,' said Pawley.

'Except for special cases,' said Dr Bee. 'Women. Administrators. Staff who've never published anything at all. They're given special consideration.'

'Anyway, they want to get rid of him,' said Henry. 'He produced a media directory of the university.'

'Well, he was in charge of the media office.'

'So he thought,' said Henry. 'He produced a directory listing all academic staff with their special expertise and research interests, so that the newspapers and radio and TV stations would know who to call up on what topic. All cross indexed and so on.'

'And?'

'It was suppressed and all copies were impounded. Then they created a new Public Relations office. All press inquiries have to go through the new office. No way they were going to let the press deal directly with individual academics. It all has to go through central control.'

'So that certain people don't get press exposure?' said Pawley.

'So that certain people don't and certain people do, and certain topics get commented on and others don't,' said Henry.

'And the directory?'

'It's been pulped.'

'Sounds like the story of one of your novels, Henry,' said Dr Bee.

They came back from lunch to find the parking area had been cordoned off and filled with sandstone blocks.

'What's all this?' asked Dr Bee.

'Sandstone blocks,' said one of the university grounds staff, standing beside a truck full of blocks and crowd barriers.

'So I see,' said Dr Bee. 'And what are they for?'

'Ah, what are they for?' said the grounds man. 'Beautification,' he said, looking Dr Bee in the eye.

'Beautification.'

'That's right, mate. Beautification of the grounds.'

'And where am I supposed to park?'

'Don't know, mate. Not here though, that's for sure.'

'You can't park here,' said one of the university police, striding over, all leather jacket and gaiters like a professor of Trans-Gender Studies.

'So where can I park?' Dr Bee pointed at his parking sticker on the windscreen. 'I pay $200 a year for parking.'

'That's not a parking permit. That's an entry permit to the university grounds.'

'But I'm allowed to park.'

'In designated areas, subject to the senate approved regulations, yes.'

'So that's just a licence to hunt for parking.'

'You could put it like that.'

He gave Dr Bee a leaflet surmounted by the embossed university crest in four colours. Report of the committee of review of parking on campus. 1). The university is committed to a policy of public transport . . . .

They drove on. Another grief too deep for words. After two fruitless circuits of the campus with not a parking spot to be found, Dr Bee took one of the twenty-five unoccupied spaces designated 'Official University vehicles only', reserved for the administrative staff who had university cars as part of their salary package. When he came to leave in the afternoon he had been wheel-clamped. It cost him a $65 on the spot payment to get the clamp removed.

'Pity you didn't have your pistol,' said Pawley. 'You could have shot it off.'

Dr Bee glowered, giving every indication that in future he would be carrying it.

'Is this a campaign to drive us out?' asked Henry,

'Yes,' said Pawley.

'Is this to make working conditions intolerable?'

'Absolutely,' said Pawley.

'What do they hope to achieve?'

'Our departure.'

Two more parking spots had been removed overnight. One had been filled with sandstone walled flower beds. The other was reserved for a rubbish skip for refuse from the animal torture laboratory in the Psychology department. Each week parking space after parking space was lost and designated for the use only of the administrative staff, the disabled, the safe from rape bus, delivery vehicles, or occupied by permanent temporary construction huts, rubbish skips and flower beds. Every week it took longer to find a parking spot, a longer cruise round the campus looking for somewhere.

'It's all a calculated part of organised harassment,' said Pawley. 'Get people to pack in the job, take early retirement, so they can replace us with non-smoking, untenured, short-term equal opportunist, culturally diverse contract staff on low wages using public transport. It's an adjunct of the 20-40-60 policy.'

'Tell me,' said Dr Bee wearily.

'Twenty-forty-sixty,' said Pawley, 'is another American initiative. It means get rid of everyone who's been here more than twenty years, is over forty, and earns over sixty thousand dollars per annum.'

'What do they want?' asked Henry.

'The hamburger university,' said Pawley. 'Staffed by ignorant smiling teenagers, painted in carefully researched colours that impel you not to linger, that drive you out rapidly so the next customer can take your place.'

As they left for lunch the painting contractors were fencing off a segment of carpark for their site hut. The Head of Department stood there beaming in her lycra gym gear and baseball hat.

'What's she doing?' snarled Dr Bee.

'The Drive-in university. She's handing out take-away assignments,' said Pawley.

'Have a nice day,' she called out to them. 'Enjoy.'

'The encouragement and fostering of mediocrity,' said Dr Bee, 'is an art. It has been known to political leaders since time immemorial. Who wants underlings who are intelligent? Who wants deputies who are more able than yourself? Every system decays as its leaders try to protect themselves by surrounding themselves with time-serving mediocrities.'

The Dead Hand, the Head of Department and Philippa went past, one behind the other, through the narrow entrance. It was actually a wide entrance but one of the double doors was always kept closed to maximise inconvenience.

'If a system like the university rewarded scholarship, how would the administrators get their way? A scholar would say, No, we cannot restructure all our courses to fit the convenience of the faculty office which has bought an inappropriate software package.'

All courses were now being restructured into three hour units because the faculty had bought an American software package programmed for three hour units. Never mind that three hour classes are too long for students' attention span. Never mind that meeting the same class two or three times a week is to meet too often and consequently the students do no preparation. That is the American model of over-teaching and the faculty office had bought it without any discussion with those who did the teaching.

'Someone with a commitment to the subject, any subject, would say, the faculty office enrolment procedures are to service academic priorities. First the teaching staff devise the courses, then the appropriate software is bought to implement them. But in this institution, no, it is the other way round, our Heads of Department advance themselves to debase the subject and to accommodate the administrators. Who in their own more elevated but exactly analogous way abase themselves to accommodate the Ministry and the Government. Whose politicians abase themselves to serve the interests of big business and the banks.'

'Usuria,' intoned Pawley.

'You ensure that your Deans and Heads of Departments know nothing, you select them on the basis of their never having produced any significant work. If they had produced the work then they would stand by it and say, No, the subject requires this. I stand by my scholarly reputation in the subject and I will not agree to these degrading, debasing and destructive changes.

'But our Deans and Heads of Department have no standing. They have never produced anything worth anything. There is nothing they can make a stand on. They go along with the administration plans because they are creatures of the administration that chose them. And it chose them for their very lack of scholarship, their very lack of production, their very lack of international, or even national, credibility, it chose them for that very mediocrity that would ensure they had no base from which to refuse the administration's demands.

'Downgrade the degree, yes, yes, yes, reduce course requirements by twenty-five per cent, yes, yes, yes.

'Remove the range of options, yes, yes, yes, reduce the range of choice for the students, yes, yes, yes, reduce the areas for staff to use or develop their expertise, yes, yes, yes.

'Slash into the MA, cut the course requirements by thirty-three per cent, yes, yes, yes.

'Abolish terms, introduce semesters, yes, yes, yes.

'These things are done with no academic or educational justification, driven by governmental imperatives of control, of accountancy, of anything but academic reason.

'What sort of academic would become a Dean, a Pro-Vice-Chancellor, a Vice-Chancellor? Only one who was no longer concerned to teach, only one who was no longer concerned to research. The people who occupy these administrative roles are self-selected failures from the academy they presume to control. They are people whose teaching skills were so derisory that they avoided teaching by getting teaching relief for administrative duties, whose ability to write or research was so inadequate that they avoided research by hiring research assistants to do their research and write their publications for them, research and publications which have no credibility in the scholarly community. These people controlling the university have no longer any day to day experience of teaching or scholarship. They are not even trained administrators, they are not even professional managers. They are the Judases of the profession, they betray what they have no skills in, they destroy the institutions in which they failed.

'And they administer with bile and resentment, encouraging their even more debased cronies in mediocrity to score off anyone who might be a threat, who might have ability, who might have intellectual quality or moral principle and consequently show them up for what they are. Those with quality are held back while the mediocre achieve accelerated promotion, those with ideas to communicate are refused research funds while those with nothing to say and a proven track record of nullity are rewarded with largesse.

'And whenever the government attempts to reduce the blowout in education costs and contain the university budgets, these are the administrators who thwart all reforms, these are the administrators who confront the demands for economies by expanding administration and reducing teaching staff, eternally protecting their own inefficiency and corruption.'

It was a tirade with no relief, no illuminating anecdotes, no parries of word play over the wine, no wit, no jokes, no sensuous pleasure of language or image, this was the burden of analysis, the unmediated message forbidden to fiction, the undiluted didacticism condemned by literary criticism, this was what had to be said and was never said and could not be said in any entertaining or engaging way. It was the irreducible, the condition and circumstance of their life.

24

The House-Sitter

Rowley had a problem. He was due to take up a visiting professorship and the tenants who were to rent his house while he was away had decided not to rent it.

'It is one of the outrages of the academic life,' said Rowley, 'that one is expected to travel, and yet one receives no proper recompense. One does one's duty in maintaining an international itinerary and yet no provision is made for the difficulties, the hardships, the expense, the trauma, yes the trauma of it all.'

'You're suggesting official house-sitters, subsidised overseas accommodation, travel loadings, business class flights, reimbursement for out of pocket expenses?' said Dr Bee.

'At the very least,' said Rowley.

'He has a point,' said Henry.

'Maybe you should draft a joint submission to the Minister of Education,' said Dr Bee.

'Yes, do that, Henry,' said Rowley. 'Send me a copy over and I'll sign it. My secretary has my address.'

Henry touched his forelock in silent acquiescence, words failing him yet again.

'But what am I going to do?' wailed Rowley. 'I can't leave the place empty.'

'Too many valuables?' said Pawley. 'The burdens of possession.'

'People just come in and vandalise,' said Rowley.

'Dinner guests do you mean?' asked Dr Bee. 'Or resentful ex-students and discarded former mistresses? One of the hazards of the job, I'm afraid. Maybe you should apply for special insurance cover. Henry could draft something about that while he's at it.'

'Just wandering drug addicts,' said Rowley.

'They could still be dinner guests, ex-students or former mistresses,' said Dr Bee.

'The price of living in the fashionable inner-city,' said Pawley.

'I can see I'm going to get no help or sympathy from you lot,' said Rowley.

'None at all,' said Dr Bee.

'None to give,' said Pawley. 'All compassion spent.'

Rowley strode off, seersucker suit strobing and distorting like American television reception, shimmering like the American flag in a desert haze of burning oil wells or pulverised mountains.

Later that day he stuck his head into Henry's room. Brett Happenstanz was there, making a few phone calls while Henry looked through his shelf of signed books to see who they could put in the international review of literature and all the arts they were planning.

Henry introduced them. 'Brett's on leave from Media Studies at Surleighwick.'

'You must visit us some time,' said Happenstanz. 'Drop in on the way to wherever you're going. We can fly you up. Always delighted to receive distinguished visitors. We could get you to do a talk.'

'I'm off at the end of the week,' said Rowley.

'What a pity I won't be there. Next time, maybe.'

The phone rang.

'For you,' said Henry, passing it across to Happenstanz.

'Yes,' said Happenstanz. 'I'm in a college guest room at the moment. Looking for somewhere more permanent. Let me know if you hear of anything.'

'That Brett Happenstanz seems a reasonable sort of chap,' said Rowley at afternoon tea.

'Seems so,' agreed Henry.

'Civilised manner.'

'Absolutely.'

'Couldn't help overhearing his phone call.'

'He has a rather penetrating phone manner,' Henry agreed.

'He's looking for somewhere to stay, I gather.'

'Apparently.'

'He'd be a reliable sort of tenant, wouldn't he?' said Rowley.

Henry was beginning to have doubts. The international review remained as evanescent as ever after months of talk. Though that was no different from the projects he'd proposed to any publisher. Anyway, it wasn't his house.

'You can always give him a try,' he said.

'He was in the same situation, he told me,' Rowley said. 'He had his apartment in London. Just put in someone to look after it, pay enough to cover the basic costs, insurance, utilities, that sort of thing. He wasn't out to make money from it, no need for a formal lease or any of that sort of thing, gentleman's agreement.'

'Perfectly house trained,' Happenstanz assured Rowley. 'Worst thing I ever did was kill a tarantula. It belonged to that old economist with the pornography collection. I was baby-sitting for him and nodded off over one of his videos - really low-grade stuff, no imagination or invention. His brat let the tarantula out of its cage and I woke up with this hideous spider sitting on my face. So I swatted it of course. He was furious. It was a pet. Said it knew him. I'm sure it did. Like knows like. But that's the worst I've ever done. Plea of self-defence.'

After which Rowley flew off in his usual inglorious blaze, being somewhere else being the American mode of academic distinction and the American mode being the only mode in town as far as Rowley was concerned.

It was some time before Rowley had the first letter from his bank. It had followed him around a bit, got delayed in the European postal networks, and Rowley was much like joy, hand ever at his lips, bidding adieu. Joy certainly bid adieu with the arrival of this communication. The cheque for the security bond Happenstanz had lodged had bounced. Or as the bank put it, they were passing it through again since there were insufficient funds in the signatory's account to meet it.

It took some further time for Rowley to make contact with Happenstanz. Apart from the initial indecision of what to do, there was the problem of time zones and the problem of catching Happenstanz when he was in and the problem of getting a phone and an international line at the right time without having to stay up half the night. This was when you needed a watch like Gervaise's navigator's special with multiple time zones on it. But when he was away Rowley liked to obliterate all consciousness of back there, that was the point of being away, and a watch with three dials would have been a constant reminder.

But reminded of it he was.

'Purely technical,' said Happenstanz at his most mellifluous, 'not to worry, temporary liquidity hitch, all taken care of. Should all have been sewn up by now. Funds deposited in a Swiss bank, that sort of thing. But there was a problem at the other end. Actually,' he said, 'you might be able to help. Expedite things. Would you like to go to Geneva? All expenses paid, of course. Stay at a top hotel. Nothing but the best. If you felt the need for a little holiday you could have this one on me and drop in at the bank. Get things moving.'

It had its tempting aspect and Rowley was the man to be tempted. But he had a little something going on down at Lake Bled and wasn't able to drag himself away.

'No problem,' said Happenstanz confidently. 'It will be sorted out in a trice. Glad you called me. I'll get on the line straight away and jolly them along. Enjoy your stay.'

'And that was the last I heard,' said Rowley.

'You didn't call him again.'

'Ah, there was a bit of a problem about that,' said Rowley, giving his charming, slightly sheepish smile. The sort that had served to get him endlessly appointed round the world. 'I was on the phone talking about *A Passage to India*. The book, I was stressing. As opposed to the film. And the wife stormed in and grabbed the mobile out of my hand and threw it into the vindaloo. I was incommunicado for a while. Lot of trouble with the rental agreement.'

'Why did she do that?' asked Dr Bee. 'She doesn't like books?'

'No, she somehow assumed I was booking a passage to the sub-continent. She said this was the last post, as it were. She was never moving anywhere else ever again. She was sick of moving. I could screw my students and research assistants till they were blue in the arse, but if I even so much as thought of applying for another job anywhere else she'd kill me first before I booked the tickets.'

'And did you?' asked Dr Bee.

'Book the tickets? No, I'm still waiting on a visa.'

'And what about turning your students' and research assistants' posteriors blue?'

'It was just a manner of speaking.'

'When I arrived back,' said Rowley, 'he met me at the airport. My car, of course, he'd had the use of that. He stopped at a bottle shop on the way home to pick up some beer. He'd just run out the night before.

'"Seem to have left my wallet back at the house,' he said."'

Rowley picked up the tab.

They sat back with a drink while Rowley relaxed from the flight, Happenstanz sucking up a beer, Rowley his duty-free bottle of wine. But it had been a long flight and Rowley soon turned in.

'I'll finish that off if you're leaving it,' said Happenstanz, reaching across for the wine.

In the morning Rowley phoned the bank. There was no record of the cheque having been deposited.

Happenstanz busied himself in the kitchen. He made them coffee.

'Only instant, I'm afraid,' he said.

Rowley's stock pile of premium Colombian coffee beans had all been gone through.

'That cheque, by the way,' said Rowley, 'did you pay it in?'

'Oh yes, sorry about that little hitch,' said Happenstanz, 'yes, that's all sorted out.'

'Do you have a deposit receipt?'

'Somewhere around,' said Happenstanz. He went off into the room he had been occupying and reappeared with a crumpled piece of paper with some digits on it.

'Seems to be it,' he said.

He handed it over to Rowley.

'Well, I'll be off,' he said. 'I think you'll find everything's in order.'

'I'll catch up with you some time,' said Rowley.

'But I never did,' said Rowley. 'And it wasn't a deposit slip. He'd never deposited anything. Then the bills started coming in. The international phone calls came to over two thousand dollars. To say nothing of the talk line calls. Phone sex.'

'Boys or girls?' asked Dr Bee.

'How would I know?' snapped Rowley.

Dr Bee raised a quizzical eyebrow. 'Sort of basic thing I'd have thought you would have known by now,' he said. 'Could get yourself into trouble if you don't.'

'The house had been drunk dry,' Rowley went on. 'Cellar drained.'

Not that anyone believed Rowley kept much of a cellar or anything else.

'Wife gets back tomorrow,' he said. 'She'll kill me if she finds out how much it's all cost.'

'It's an ill wind that blows no good,' said Dr Bee.

Dr Bee turned up a lead. He came into the common room with a xerox of a newspaper report of Happenstanz's arrest six months earlier.

'Where did you get this?' said Rowley. 'How did you find this?'

'The secretary in the departmental office, actually,' said Dr Bee. 'Apparently he's quite well known.'

Rowley skimmed through the paragraphs.

'You mean this whole time he's been out on bail awaiting trial?'

'So it says,' said Dr Bee.

'What did he do?' asked Henry.

'He got himself a lectureship at the University of Surleighwick on the basis of degrees he said he had but didn't. Printed up phoney certificates.'

'So he wasn't an academic at all?' said Rowley.

'Yes he was,' said Dr Bee.

'He was a fake.'

'No, the degrees were faked, but he was a real academic. As real as they come. The university appointed him and he did the job. He probably did it better than those with so called authentic degrees. Almost certainly.'

'Very creative chap,' said Henry. 'Lots of people skills. Absolutely charming. I knew all along he was the right person to run a literary review.'

'You knew this, Henry?' Rowley fumed.

'Can't say I ever had firm evidence. Fooled me as much as you.'

'Fooled?' said Rowley. 'I've been robbed.'

'Always more expensive than you expect, these overseas jaunts,' said Dr Bee.

'Think of Henry's international review of all the arts,' said Pawley. 'Funded by Castro's mistress. Head office in Paris. Readings in the Albert Hall. All come to nothing, all up in smoke.'

'It's an ill wind that blows no good,' said Dr Bee yet once more.

25

Better Dead Than Red

The faculty club buzzed with excitement. Old Bannerman in History had been found shot dead in his room. The usually morgue like atmosphere of the club blossomed with a living death. At last something had happened.

'Apparently he had a habit of being in his room late at night,' Edwina was saying. 'What he used to do, who knows? He'd been getting more and more difficult. I must say I think it was probably the best thing. It has saved us from having to make some very painful decisions.'

'I'd have thought a bullet through the head would have been pretty painful,' said Pawley.

Edwina scowled at him. 'It was very distressing for the attendants. It was a typically thoughtless act. You'd have thought that even he could have shot himself in his own house.'

'What sort of weapon was it?' asked Dr Bee.

Edwina looked at him with horror and distaste. They all looked at him with horror and distaste.

'I really have no idea.'

'It would be interesting to know,' said Dr Bee.

Bannerman had been an old leftie. A communist all his life. It had been a life of increasing isolation, as his comrades either died or deserted and History, the department of, left him to one side. In the early years of the Cold War he had published prolifically. Those had been the good old days.

'Of course we were embattled, but we had our supporters. Of course the right was trying to destroy us and discredit us and blacklist us, but that was because we were significant. We had a movement. We had a following. People wanted to read committed scholarship.'

He would talk to Pawley when they bumped into each other around the university. He wasn't somebody who always had to rush off. He had time to sit over a non-decaffeinated coffee, light up a forbidden cigarette, share sad observations.

'Now it's all different,' he said. 'Now the left has lost critical mass. They're picking us off one by one.'

He was an obvious candidate for a chair in terms of his scholarship and publications, but in the years when he had bothered to apply some rumour was always circulated, some lie disseminated, and he was always blocked. He was an obvious candidate for a personal chair but he was as effectively blocked there.

'There is no doubt about your publication record,' Edwina told him, 'in the past. But it is not only a matter of that. Graduate students, for instance. You don't list any graduate students you have supervised. Have you had any? How many?'

'No idea,' he said. 'I've never thought to keep a list. It's just part of the job. Why would I keep a list?'

'Well, that's one of your problems,' Edwina told him.

The other problem, which he didn't bother to elaborate on, was that the department kept graduate students away from him.

No matter that his reputation was world-wide. No matter that his work was cited endlessly. Or maybe that was the matter. He was a threat. He had published too much. He was recognised too widely. He showed up the idleness and mediocrity of his colleagues just by his own production and they never forgave him for it. Besides which, he didn't have a doctorate himself.

'In my day,' he said, 'a doctorate was the mark of failure. If you were any good you got snapped up for a fellowship or a lectureship as soon as you graduated. You might have enrolled as a graduate student, but if you showed any ability you were given a job. The people who completed their PhDs were the ones no one would employ. They were the only ones left doing graduate work.'

It was not the sort of comment that endeared him to his doctored colleagues.

'Your day was a long time ago,' they told him, 'and now it is over.'

And indeed his day had passed. His publications dropped off. It wasn't that he wasn't still productive.

'The older you are the wiser you get,' he assured Pawley. 'Unless you go ga-ga and they certainly try and make you go that way. Decent cultures respect age and intellect. Look at the Chinese. Age is seen as bringing wisdom and wisdom is what you can impart as a teacher. And what do we do? We run a campaign of early retirement and attempt to drive anybody who knows anything or who's thought about anything out of the university.'

But the new times didn't want the wisdom of the left. The publishers he used to publish with were bought up by the big conglomerates and their lists purged. The end of history, the end of ideology, the end of grand narratives, their editors parroted.

He kept on writing.

'When you've been around long enough the requests start coming in from memorial volumes and festschrifts. Always someone you know retiring or dying, always someone putting together some collection in their honour. Keeps you in business.'

He still had contacts scattered round the world. The essays still appeared in unreconstructed scholarly journals and in short-lived enthusiastic ventures in oppositional polemic. But there were fewer such journals. And the days when he could collect these pieces into volume form had gone, and the volumes of collections that he had published went out of print and there were no more paperback editions.

And the university proceeded with its own restructuring. New rules came in. Minimum enrolment for courses. And his courses were no longer in the vanguard. The vanguard now was 'Cross-dressing in History,' 'The Development of the Gay Mardi Gras in the 1990s,' 'Women Travellers since 1968,' 'Time, Space and the Body.'

'Is this History?' he asked.

They thought it was.

The theoreticians revised the syllabus and proclaimed the liberation of History from the tyranny of content.

He roared with laughter and left the meeting.

'These are the days of grand hypocrisy,' he told Pawley. 'Our new guardians of History have announced that since fifty per cent of the world's population are women, then fifty per cent of the content of every course must be Women's History. Not fifty per cent of the courses even, but fifty per cent of every course taught. I pointed out that fifty per cent of the world's population lived in Asia so by that argument fifty per cent of our courses should have an Asian content. Not to mention an Asian language component.'

But they had the last laugh. They closed down his courses because the enrolments did not meet the new quotas they had established.

They gave him twelve first year tutorials and told him to go for retraining at the Centre of Profitable Teaching.

'I am not going to be retrained at my age,' he said.

The Head of Department instructed him to go for counselling.

He refused that too.

They refused him stationery and photocopying.

'Photocopying is free only for teaching. If you are copying for research then it has to be paid for from a research grant.'

'I don't have a research grant.'

'Then you must apply for one.'

'Why should I apply for one? I've written twenty-five books without ever applying for a research grant or using a research assistant, why should I start now?'

'It's up to you. If you want stationery you have to supply it.'

He took out a classified advertisement in the *University Mirror*. 'Exchange one swivelling Associate-Professorial adjustable chair for equivalent value in A4 stationery.'

'Why would I apply for a research grant?' he asked Pawley. 'The whole scheme is a criminal scandal. Besides which,' he said, 'and more to the immediate point, I wouldn't get one. Between you and me and this bugged lamp post, I've applied before and always been refused. They send my project out for assessment to my various enemies and they shaft me. Every time.'

'I got knocked back too,' said Pawley.

'Of course you would. What's the point in having a grants scheme unless you can blacklist people?'

He had begun speaking openly and often about enemies. What he said was undoubtedly true. But it made him sound mad. And that was what his enemies intended.

'Only one thing they hate more than dead white males,' he said, 'and that's living red males. But they're working on it, never you doubt it, they're working on it, of that I'm sure.'

So there he was, eight hours of first year tutorials a week. In one way it didn't matter. He was philosophical about that. Whatever the course, whatever the syllabus, he brought to it his own brand of class analysis.

The students complained. Not to him.

'That is the significant thing,' he said to Pawley. 'No one has said anything to me. But some organised lobby group has complained to the complaints tribunal. We have an official complaints tribunal to shaft people like me. They complain I use words they don't understand, like ideology and dialectical. They complain I talk about class. Familiar, somewhat? They complain I set them too much to read. They complain that they can't understand my accent.'

He had no doubt that it was an organised campaign.

'There are the bonuses, too,' he said. 'Nubile little girls who come and rub up against you. Waiting for the ill-considered response that will produce a sexual harassment charge. But you can't catch an old bird like me with chaff.'

Pawley had not been so sure. If they wanted to catch him there was no doubt in Pawley's mind that they would. Now it seemed that they had.

'All the same,' said Pawley, 'I'm surprised he killed himself. They were targeting him without a doubt. But he was used to that. He'd been targeted all his life. He used to say he was like a walnut tree, the more they beat him the stronger he grew.'

'There are precedents,' said Henry, who had been researching literary deaths. 'Radicals have killed themselves before. V. Gordon Childe. Jack London.'

'I've never been convinced about either of those cases,' said Pawley. 'Did Childe jump off the Blue Mountains or was he pushed? Did Jack London really write down calculations of a lethal dose of morphine before shooting himself up, or did somebody do it for him? Why calculate, why not just whack it all in? Same with Abby Hoffman, I think they shot him up. Bobby Seale, shot him down. Jerry Rubin, ran him over. Never been convinced about Shelley, either. Was it just a sailing accident? And we know they poisoned Andrew Marvell.'

'The reason I asked what sort of pistol he used, which seems to have so shocked our rarely so sensitive colleagues -' said Dr Bee.

'Shocked me,' admitted Henry.

'Is not because I am a pistol freak -'

'Never thought it for a minute,' said Pawley.

'But because it is not that easy to kill yourself with a small gun. You have to know what you're doing.'

'You mean a .22 is the mark of a contract killer,' said Pawley.

'My word, you are well informed on these things for a semi-professional vegetarian pacifist,' said Dr Bee.

'I can't imagine Edwina went in there herself and pulled the trigger,' said Henry.

'Well -' said Pawley.

'Nor can I imagine the university took out a contract.'

'The failure of the novelist's imagination yet once more,' said Dr Bee.

'But I'm certainly willing to believe that she and her appointed hirelings in history harassed him to such an extent that suicide seemed a welcome option.'

'We can all believe that,' said Dr Bee. 'I don't think that stretches anyone's powers of imagination.'

'Could happen to any of us,' said Pawley.

26

Student Assessment

The semester crept its desultory way to its unsatisfactory end, signalling a pervasive sense of futility. The mid-semester break had been set three-quarters of the way through the semester, as ever. It was one of the regular destructive absurdities no one even thought to question any more. It meant that by the time it came everyone was exhausted, staff and students alike. On top of which there was the usual uncertainty about whether the break was one or two weeks, some people extending it to two weeks by offering a 'reading week.' But some reading weeks were the week before the break, some the week after, with the consequence that the majority of students took off the week before the break, the break, and the week after the break. And after that they never felt like returning, since there were only two or three weeks of the semester left after the break. And no one ever knew whether it was another two or another three weeks that the semester continued. Officially the semesters were fifteen weeks, but that was subverted by a rule of teaching only fourteen weeks, and the Arts faculty had its own rule, or used to, of teaching thirteen weeks. The rule may have been rescinded but no one seemed to know. So the semester always ended in uncertainty and unsatisfactoriness, and every year Henry was outraged to find he was turning up to classes only to find Gervaise and the Head of Department had closed theirs down two weeks earlier.

'I thought I was cutting it fine, shaving off a week, but those scoundrels -'

'You stand amazed at your own moderation yet again,' said Dr Bee.

'I do indeed.'

'What annoys me,' said Pawley, 'is there's always likely to be one or two students who turn up. If they'd all just stay away it would be much easier.'

And now the Head of Department added to the sense of dissatisfaction with a circular informing everyone that the new course assessment questionnaires designed by the Centre of Profitable Teaching were available for distribution.

'This,' said Henry, 'is the final indignity.'

''Tis not the end when we can say this is the end,' Dr Bee reminded him.

'Why should I be assessed by my students?'

'Because the Head of Department in this as in all else is in complicity with the administration and the administration wants instruments to control, destabilise and ultimately get rid of us,' said Pawley. 'Her mission in what is laughingly called her life is to spread wretchedness and misery.

'What do they think will be gained?' said Henry.

'Desperation, more retirements, more sticks to beat us with,' said Pawley. 'It's just one more piece of American control they've imported. It's something they can threaten you with. Well, Mr Lancaster, over fifty per cent of your students graded you a failure, what do you say to that? Will you take a retraining course at the Centre of Profitable Teaching, or retirement by the end of the year, which do you favour?'

The student responses were gems of incisiveness and rigour. 'Two hours is too long for a class. Why can't we have a coffee break in the middle?' 'The lecturer talks too quickly.' 'There is too much to read.'

'Look at these,' said Henry, sifting through the responses.

'I refuse,' said Dr Bee.

'We're supposed to read them and comment on them,' said Henry.

'That's the Head of Department's own little twist of the knife,' said Dr Bee. 'Who wants to read what they write? I can tell you what their responses are. How many A grades did you give for the first assignment, Henry?'

'I don't know, let me find my mark sheet.'

'Oh, don't be pedantic, just give me a number.'

'Eight, say.'

'And how many Bs?'

'Oh, about fourteen.'

'And how many failures?'

'A couple.'

'So,' said Dr Bee, 'Abracadabra, eight students will assess you A, fourteen will assess you B, and two will assess you as a failure. Am I not right?'

Henry leafed through the assessments.

'You are right.'

'How can it be otherwise?' asked Dr Bee. 'What students will give you an A if you gave them a B? Who will pass you when you have failed them? The whole process is an entirely predictable waste of time.'

'No,' said Pawley. 'It's not a waste of time as far as the Head of Department and her cronies are concerned. It's an incentive to degradation. And that's what they want. What you do is you give everyone As and you get an award for teaching excellence. It's one more way to institutionalise corruption and debase standards. A triumph of managerialism.'

'So what do I do?' said Henry. 'We're supposed to read them and hand them over to the Head of Department with our comments.'

'Just write "not good enough,"' said Dr Bee.

'That's too provocative,' said Pawley. 'I just wrote "satisfactory."'

'Were they?'

'No idea. Couldn't face looking at them.'

'What about yours?' Henry asked Dr Bee.

'Oh, I didn't have any,' said Dr Bee. 'Usual end of semester situation. Only a couple of students turned up so I sent them off to the library. And then there was no point handing out questionnaires with no one there.'

Henry looked aghast.

'Just throw them in the wastepaper bin,' Dr Bee advised him, 'and say no one turned up. Who's to know? Who's to care?'

'I can't do that.'

'Well you can't put in those pathetic responses. If you're going to hand something in at least get some blank forms and fill them in yourself with something positive. Creative writing, Henry. Be creative, isn't that what it's all about?'

The students may have given up coming to class but they still romped around the campus on skateboards as if it were one big playground.

'Here are your assessors,' said Dr Bee. 'These be your gods, oh Israel. In the past undergraduates attempted to be adult. They tried to appear older than their years. It made them pretentious and presumptuous but it was better than this return to primary school. You never see a briefcase any more. Now they all wear school satchels on their backs like mentally disadvantaged seven year olds.'

'That way they can swing round in the corridors and knock you to the ground with them,' said Pawley. 'Give them a wide berth is my advice.'

As they drove out for lunch they were delayed by a troop of students with coloured chalks, crawling on their hands and knees across the roadway, tongues sticking out as they laboriously and lovingly coloured in letters announcing an end of semester kindergarten party.

'Remember when it used to be political slogans?' said Pawley.

'The Centre of Profitable Teaching encourages this,' said Dr Bee.

'Is that who supplies the coloured chalk?' said Henry.

'All that guff they disseminate about the necessity of course descriptions. It's making it all like a school. Spell out in simple words what the course is about, what the aims are, what are the intentions, what will be the outcomes.'

'I just put "to subvert bourgeois ideology,"' said Pawley.

'And they printed it in the handbook?' asked Henry.

'Oddly enough, no,' said Pawley. 'They managed to leave the course out altogether.'

'I used to think the job would last my lifetime,' said Dr Bee. 'Now I'm not so sure.'

There were no alternatives. They had combed them through endlessly, lunch after lunch. They had no skills that anyone wanted. They were superfluous men. They were not even like politicians who had been voted out of office, like former presidents of the United States, who may never have worked in their life but at least had lots of contacts someone might find useful.

'Media,' said Lancaster. 'Not a hope, Gervaise is always going on about getting a little job in publishing. There are no jobs. The whole industry has been purged. Mass sackings. They only employ youngsters now and sack them when they've used them up.'

'They sack them as soon as they start to know what's going on,' said Pawley. 'The basic agenda is to purge the press and television of the left. Under the guise of economic rationalisation.'

'Doesn't matter what your politics are,' said Lancaster. 'We're too old.'

'Exactly,' said Pawley. 'We're too old to be pushed around and eat shit any more.'

'I've never noticed that in this institution,' said Dr Bee. 'Age has never been a bar to servility and sycophancy in the university.'

'What about the church?' Lancaster mused. 'There must be jobs there. Some cosy little bishopric.'

'I don't think you can just move across to the top,' said Pawley. 'you'd have to do an apprenticeship as a curate in an AIDS hospice or something.'

'Not on,' said Henry.

'Should've gone in the army,' said Pawley. 'Then we'd be out on a pension running a caravan park up the coast.'

'With full weapons training,' agreed Dr Bee.

'What about the fashion business?' said Pawley.

He gestured across the road. The windows of the boutique opposite were pasted over with signs announcing CLOSING DOWN SALE and FOR LEASE. The doors were closed, the shop empty of stock, the girls had gone, no longer prancing and posing and posturing.'

'Maybe this is the end after all,' conceded Dr Bee.

27

The Raising of the Curtains

Pawley had been a scholar, or one part of him had, not that long ago. A thousand and one joints ago. At ten a day that was only four months. Longer than that. Longer than that indeed. Indeed the last four months had seen a recuperation of interest in scholarship. At least he was still in the game, as the profession called it.

'Homo ludens, you know,' Henry would add, in explanation.

Pawley himself didn't think of it as a game. A racket, a scam, a lurk, an easy option, better than working, but not a game, he didn't see games as any of those things, games were things designed to divert your attention from reality. Rackets and scams and lurks released you to pay more attention to it. Reality.

And it wasn't that easy. Some who'd tried to make it really easy had cracked altogether. Begun by taking all the leave due to them. Then long service leave. Even unpaid leave. Then a bit of moonlighting, another job or two. And then they'd lost their balance altogether, crashing down like uncertain cyclists. They'd cleared out their rooms, more or less, sent in their resignations to the registrar from interstate, and left behind a few books they hadn't sold off and a cactus or a rag doll or two left shoes, something symbolic for their remaining colleagues to ponder on.

Well, he hadn't come into an inheritance or amassed impossible debts or decided to become a full-time writer. He didn't want to be a full-time anything.

'Well, you're semi-retired anyway, aren't you?' his laundryman said.

At least that must have meant that he must seem at last semi-participant. A semi-detached scholar. It sounded very petty-bourgeois.

'All these years of aspiration and all I've reached is the petty bourgeoisie,' he complained at one departmental meeting. Apropos what he couldn't remember. Alienation was too long a word for it.

Pawley wasn't exactly a victim of the sixties. He resisted the idea of being classified as a victim even more than being a victim. Most of the sixties he had been too drunk to notice them. It was only when he couldn't face the hangovers with their long retching haul through till four in the afternoon before something like tolerable life was regained that he turned to the sixties which had already gone. Indeed it could be said that the sixties saved him from alcoholism. Or the seventies did. He said so, anyway. Sometimes.

He went out into the yard and picked off the remaining leaves and half formed heads from the sad consumed marijuana plant in its pot. He had given up meat out of sympathy for the victim, but he really had to stop empathising with the marijuana plant. Anyway, it had to go. He'd try and clean the place up before Harbinger arrived. He didn't know if he could handle it without dope but he'd try. He really would.

Just out of the blue, the cerulean blue above the white domes, what white domes, just out of the blue, as far as he could recall, this letter from Harbinger had arrived saying he would be just passing through and had an overnight stop and if it was no inconvenience or trouble possibly they might meet.

Harbinger had been his tutor. Back in the days when the world was wide. Once or twice he'd seen him in the intervening years. A nice man. Not that he felt he'd ever known him especially well. Or had he? If these stoned days at the end of the world seemed alienated, then what were those times at Oxford like? Weird. It all seemed terribly weird. He felt sick on the stomach with empathy for his earlier self. Roll another smoke. Once he would have put on a record but he hadn't replaced the stereo since the last time he was burgled. One morning we'll wake up and find rock music no longer has anything to say to us. Something like that. The line of a poem. Maybe this was the morning. A different sort of poem from the ones he'd discussed with Harbinger. He could see it could all be an awful disaster if he wasn't careful. And he didn't think that he was especially: careful. That was one of the problems. He ripped the poor young plant bodily out of its pot. That could be seen as being careful but he wasn't sure that it was. He'd end up smoking it all and have nothing left for when he needed it, for when Harbinger came.

Harbinger didn't seem any different from twenty years ago. The soles of his shoes no longer had holes in them, at least this pair didn't, but they were the same sort of shoes, anonymous black shoes that probably had a style name though Pawley wasn't sure of it. They ought to have been Oxfords, but were they? The same grey suit, crumpled as ever. The same ageless, indeterminate look, vaguely middle aged but with a twenty year leeway on either side of what you might hazard a guess that it was. The same quiet, tentative manner.

'What I don't have time to do,' Harbinger said, 'is get to your library.'

'It's not a bad library,' said Pawley.

'No, not at all,' said Harbinger. 'In fact it has some very interesting items. Very interesting.'

'Yes,' said Pawley. He was sure it did.

'What I wanted to do,' said Harbinger, 'or what I'd promised to do, to be more precise, was look at a book that used to be in Dr Dee's library.'

'The magician?'

'Well, the Elizabethan Magus.'

'Didn't know we had any books of his,' said Pawley.

'Just the one.'

'I wonder how we got it. I thought his library had been burned by an angry mob.'

'Well, no. You're quite right, that was the story, but it seems now that wasn't the case. But a lot of his books were removed by government agents.'

'And this was one of them.'

'Possibly. As I said, I wasn't able to get to see it.'

'What's the book we've got? Is it interesting?'

'Not really,' said Harbinger. 'No, the interest lies in its being Dee's. He had this habit of marking his books.'

'What sort of markings?'

'Oh, little signs and sigils. Lines. That sort of thing.'

'And you're working on this?'

'No, not at all, heaven forbid,' said Harbinger. He fumbled in his tobacco pouch like a koala cracking fleas. 'No, not my sort of thing. Fellow I know is assembling an inventory of the surviving books, though. When he heard I was coming out here he asked if I could have a look at it for him.'

'But you're not going to have time to do it now.'

'Not now they've messed up the flight times.'

'Could I do it for you?' said Pawley.

'Well,' said Harbinger.

Memories of happy days of scholarship in the upper reading room flooded back momentarily. The roar of B-52s overhead.

'Well, don't go to a lot of trouble about it,' Harbinger said. 'I don't want to take up your time.'

'I've plenty of time,' said Pawley.

Harbinger pursed his lips.

'You better tell me what sort of signs and sigils.'

'Well, anything,' said Harbinger.

Pawley walked across the lawns to the library. Once they would have been packed with protesting students. Chewing their sandwiches while they pondered direct action. Wanted activists would appear and make impassioned harangues and daring getaways. And special branch would photograph them from high buildings or just walk amongst them as if they were taking souvenir shots of happy days. Now it was just empty lawns. The calm and discretion of an up-market cemetery. Or an empty theme park, waiting for a theme.

A bus load of schoolgirls was parked there and the girls were shouting out to two or three students throwing books down from the library roof.

'Jump,' they called. 'Jump, go on, jump.'

He went into the inner recesses of the building to the rare book room and ordered the Dee volume. The librarian went into further recesses, carrying the call number on a scrap of paper. Pawley read through the record book of who had ordered up what as he waited. *Boy and Girl Tramps in America*. A hitherto unknown interest of one of his colleagues.

The librarian came back up and looked at him and went away again. After a while another librarian came in with the scrap of paper.

'I'll just check the call number again, if you don't mind.'

'Isn't it there?' said Pawley, premature as always, ascribing error and failure to yet another institution all too readily.

'What was the title again?' asked the librarian, ignoring Pawley's question.

He pulled out the catalogue drawer and looked at the card and looked at the scrap of paper and didn't add anything.

'Did I get it right?' Pawley asked.

The librarian smiled a thin smile.

'We'll see.'

Time passed in this timeless zone. The conditioned air circulated like well-drilled legionnaires. The librarian re-emerged from the inner sanctum.

'What, ah, what were you wanting this for?'

'Just to have a look at it,' said Pawley.

'Yes,' said the librarian, 'yes, yes, of course. Is there any special, ah, reason?'

'It used to belong to Dr Dee,' said Pawley. 'The Elizabethan Magus.'

'Yes, yes, yes, of course.'

'It has his signature on the title page,' said Pawley. 'Apparently. I haven't actually seen it yet.'

'Ah,' said the librarian. 'And you wanted to see that. Of course. Ah.'

He went across to a glass fronted bookcase against the wall. It was locked. He went back to his desk and took a key from a little cardboard box.

They were all old, leather bindings, some of them scuffed, most of them with gold lettering. He read along their spines, Pawley looking over his shoulder. It wasn't among them. Once again the librarian disappeared.

When he came back again it was with yet another librarian. She looked at Pawley first before doing anything else, as if to see what could be causing so much trouble and hoping maybe it would evaporate under her gaze. Then she sat down at the desk and drew a little portable card-index box across to her, sifting through the cards with long meticulous fingers. Then she took a key from another cardboard box and went to the display case against the wall. The other librarian followed. Pawley watched them.

She opened one of the doors and took down a book from its stand. It was open at its title page. She locked the cabinet door and brought the book back to the desk, opening it at the title page again for him. There it was, Johannes Dee, along the top of the ruled border. Pawley tried to summon up the appropriate thanks and pack away all the ever ready, anti-bureaucratic, anti-institutional, anti-librarian, anti-life rage that had been assembling in a rough and ready way for some rough and ready use. But she simply moved the line of her mouth into the horizontal, momentarily, before letting it settle back into the hemispheric downturn of discontent and then she was gone, leaving the book on the duty librarian's desk and the duty librarian standing there, waiting for the book to be taken off his desk to one of the readers' desks.

'Marvellous,' said Pawley.

'Could you fill in the register?' said the librarian. Before you look at it, was what his toneless tone insisted. Authority reasserted, reinstated.

Pawley filled it in and took the book off to one of the desks. It seemed to be a collection of mathematical tables. Columns of figures. Totally incomprehensible to Pawley. But on one or two pages there were ink markings. Brief lines in the margins. He put little scraps of marker paper in each page where there was a mark, and went back through it a couple of times in case he'd missed any. The scholar. What a vocation he could have had. Then he took it back to the duty librarian and asked if he could get those pages copied.

'It will have to be photographed. We can't photocopy these old books. It damages the bindings pressing them flat.'

'That's all right,' said Pawley.

'It might take a little time,' said the duty librarian.

'Ah well,' said Pawley.

'And I'll need your library card and your requisition number.'

'Sure.'

'What size prints will you require?'

He had no idea, but he studied the permutations available and borrowed the ruler from the desk and measured and calculated and in the end there was nothing else that the librarian seemed able to think of, and Pawley thanks him, and scuttled out into the bright light of the afternoon, and the empty lawns and the cloudless sky and the renewed vacuity of diurnal existence.

Now that his researches into hashish and literature had failed to secure a grant, and indeed had come to seem injudicious, there wasn't that much call to use the library. A month or more had passed before he thought about the Dr Dee prints. Nothing had arrived. He dragged himself across to the rare book room one afternoon, sweating through the humidity, into the air-conditioned coolness.

'I ordered some prints some time ago.'

'Yes,' said the duty librarian.

'I wondered if they'd arrived yet.'

'Arrived?' said the librarian.

'Yes.'

'Arrived where?'

'Well, here.'

'Were they supposed to have arrived here?' the librarian asked, that familiar sceptical note, lips pursed in distaste.

'I can't remember whether I was to pick them up here or they were to be sent to me.'

'They wouldn't be here,' said the librarian. 'We don't make them here. We send everything to photography.'

'I know,' said Pawley. 'I just wondered what happened to them.'

'You'd have to ask photography.'

It was a large campus and photography was some distance from the library. He put it off till another day, no point in going in the afternoon, who knew how early they shut? But when he went there, another day, giving himself time in the morning before the commitments of lunch, they didn't know anything about it.

'What was the job number?'

He gave them the job number.

'No, that's your departmental requisition number, we need a job number.'

'I can't remember,' he said.

'Well, what was the job then?'

'It was a rare book.'

'They're all rare to hear them talk. What was it called?'

He had no idea what it was called. Some *Tractatus* or other. It was the signature and annotations he wanted copied, not the book itself. Always the periphery, never the substance.

'Can't help you, mate. If you haven't got a job number and you don't know what the book's called, how are we going to find out what it is, we aren't, are we?'

A door behind reception opened and he glimpsed four or five white overalled technicians throwing dice.

'Your best bet is to ask them at the library.'

He went back there, back to the library, went through it all again. He looked at the display case but it was a different display. The duty librarian disappeared yet once more into the bowels and the rare book librarian came in again, gave him her standard hard look, took out the bunch of keys and unlocked the cabinet in the room there. There were a number of books lying flat in the cupboard, slips of paper sticking out from between the leaves. She took them out, put them on the desk, carefully opened them one by one. He stood there watching from the other side of the desk.

'That's it,' he said, 'that's it, I think.' The signature written along the top of the title page border. It was upside down from where he stood so he couldn't be sure, but it was a signature.

She put it aside, put the other books away, locked them up, handed it to him, tight-lipped, silent, and went to head off again.

'But the prints?' Pawley asked.

'Prints?' she said.

'I ordered prints.'

'It would have to go to photography for prints,' she said.

'But that's what I wanted,' she said.

'Oh,' she said, 'You'll have to fill in a requisition for that.'

'I already have.'

She opened the book and looked at the title page.

'About a month ago.'

She sat down at the desk, opened a drawer, took out a folder of pink flimsy dockets, leafed through them backwards, one by one, and then forwards, one by one.

'There's nothing here,' she said.

He suppressed a groan, turned it into his smoker's cough.

'Perhaps you should fill out one now.'

He gave it another month before he tried again. The rare book librarian offered a smile of recognition.

'Did you get your prints?'

'No, that's what I came over for.'

She looked puzzled.

'Are you sure?'

'Yes, quite sure.'

'Oh,' she said, 'that's strange. Because photography have sent the book back.'

She unlocked the cupboard, took out the stack of books, old bindings, there it was.

'Perhaps you should -'

'Try photography?'

'Yes. Yes, that would probably be the thing to do.'

'Tell you what,' said the man in photography, resplendent in his spotless white boiler suit, holding the pink flimsy out at arm's length and squinting at it and running his finger down the columns of the job book, 'tell you what, I remember seeing it, it was an old book, right? One of them rare ones, right, I remember it because we don't get much call for them, mainly medical work we do here, tissues and growths, all the creepy-crawly stuff, you know, so an old book sort of stands out, and I remember it in the out tray. What must have happened was it came in and somehow it got put in the out tray and it got sent back without ever getting done. See, there's no records of it being done, get what I mean, but I do remember seeing it, an old book, you say, it was sitting there in the out tray, I'm almost certain, mind you I couldn't swear to it, but. . . .'

'Back again?' said the librarian. 'How did it go?'

'It didn't,' said Pawley. 'They put it in the out tray and never did it.'

'How extraordinary,' said the librarian. 'Makes you think it doesn't want to be photographed, doesn't it? The revenge of Dr Dee.'

'It does seem like it,' said Pawley.

'Maybe it has a spell on it.'

'Just what I need,' said Pawley.

She looked at him, waiting.

'So what should I do now?'

She carried on looking.

'Fill out another form?'

'I'm afraid you'll have to,' she said.

'The first time it never even reached photography,' Pawley said.

'Yes, well, that does seem to have been our fault.'

He waited.

'Perhaps it would be best if you took it over yourself. It's breaking all the rules, but -' she shrugged - 'the rules don't seem to be helping very much. If you left me your borrower's card . . .'

She escorted Pawley out through the security check at the door.

'If you could just get them to phone to confirm they have it when you arrive,' she said, 'and then I can let you have your card back and then. . . .' She smiled. 'Well, then we'll see.'

He carried the package in a brown paper envelope across the campus. It seemed to be pulsing under his arm. He took especial care not to get hit by passing cars, bowled over by students on skate-boards and mobile telephones. He got it there.

'Third time lucky is it?' said the white boiler-suited man. 'Wouldn't think an old thing like this had so much life in him, would you?'

'Makes you wonder,' said Pawley at afternoon tea, replenishing the liquid he had sweated out walking back and forward across campus.

'Does it?' said Dr Bee.

'Makes you wonder if it's something Dr Dee didn't want copied.'

Dr Bee looked at him sceptically. 'And he emailed his request through to rare books from beyond the grave?'

'I was thinking more in terms of magic,' said Pawley. 'A spell.'

'A spell.'

'Well, it's pretty extraordinary. All those attempts and still not copied.'

'With photography and the library involved,' said Dr Bee, 'it would only be magic if the prints were ever made.'

But Pawley resisted. The curtains of the dark had been momentarily raised. He gave silent thanks to Dr Dee. There was another reality. Somewhere. He had to believe that. Otherwise it was all insupportable.

MICHAEL WILDING

IS AUTHOR OF A DOZEN VOLUMES OF FICTION INCLUDING

Living Together (UQP), *The Short Story Embassy* (Wild & Woolley), *The Paraguayan Experiment* (Penguin), *The Man of Slow Feeling* (Penguin), *Under Saturn* (Black Swan), *Great Climate* (Faber) and most recently *Wildest Dreams* (UQP) and *Raising Spirits, Making Gold and Swapping Wives: the True Adventures of Dr John Dee and Sir Edward Kelly* (Shoestring), one of the *Economist's* Books of the Year.

His literary studies include *Political Fictions* (Routledge), *Marcus Clarke* (Oxford University Press), *Dragons Teeth: Literature in the English Revolution* (Clarendon Press) and *Studies in Classic Australian Fiction* (Sydney Studies). He edited *The Tabloid Story Pocket Book* (Wild & Woolley) and *The Oxford Book of Australian Short Stories* (Oxford).

MICHAEL WILDING has taught literature and creative writing at the University of Birmingham, the University of California at Santa Barbara, the National University of Singapore, and the University of Sydney, where he is now Emeritus Professor.

MICHAEL WILDING's books can be purchased on-line from the NSW Writers' Centre Bookstore at www.nswwriterscentre.org.au